The Ivory Cane

Janet Dailey

AN [*e-reads*] BOOK
New York, NY

Copyright © 1977 by Janet Dailey
First e-reads publication 2004
www.e-reads.com
ISBN 0-7592-5746-9

Table of Contents

One

Overhead a sea gull screeched. The blustery wind off the Pacific Ocean swirled around the boats docked at the Yacht Harbor of San Francisco Bay. Distantly came the clang of a cable car, the one climbing the steep hill of Hyde Street.

A light blue Continental with a leather-grained top of dark blue was wheeled expertly into the parking lot in front of the harbor. The driver, a stunningly beautiful, titian-haired woman in her mid-thirties, braked the car precisely between the white parking lines and switched off the motor. As she reached for the door handle, emerald green eyes flicked to the silent girl in the passenger seat.

'It's quite chilly outside, Sabrina. It probably would be best if you waited in the car while I see if your father is back.' It was a statement, not a suggestion that the woman made.

Sabrina Lane opened her mouth to protest. She was tired of being treated as an invalid. With a flash of insight, she realized that Deborah was not concerned about her health as much as she was about spending some time alone with Sabrina's father.

'Whatever you say, Deborah,' she submitted grudgingly, her right hand closing tightly over the smooth handle of her oak cane.

The silent moments following Deborah's departure grated at Sabrina's already taut nerves. It was difficult enough to endure her own physical restrictions without having her father's girlfriend place others on her, regardless of the motive.

Her father's girlfriend. One corner of her wide mouth turned up wryly at the phraseology. Her father had had many women friends since her mother died when Sabrina was seven. But Deborah Mosley was not just another woman. If it had not been for Sabrina's

1

accident some eight months ago, Deborah would have already been her new stepmother.

Prior to the accident, Sabrina had thought it was terrific that her father had found someone he wanted to marry. Deborah Mosley wouldn't have been Sabrina's choice, although she liked her, but that hadn't mattered not as long as her father was happy.

That was before the accident, when Sabrina had been totally independent. She had had a place of her own, a very small apartment, but it had been hers. She had had a career, not a lucrative one, but she could have supported herself.

Now — the word screamed with its own despairing wail. It would be a long time, if ever, before Sabrina could say any of that again.

'Why me?' a sobbing, self-pitying voice asked silently. 'What did I ever do to deserve this? Why me?'

Her throat tightened with pain at the unanswerable question. There was simply too much time to think. Too much time to think about the 'what-might-have-beens' and the 'if-onlys.' The damage was done and irreparable, as specialist after specialist had told Sabrina and her father. She would be incapacitated for the rest of her life and there was nothing, barring a miracle, that could ever be done to change it.

A seed of rebellion stirred to life. An anger seethed to the surface that she might forever sit in cars and stay at home while someone else decided what was best for her.

A sickening thought sprang to mind. Suppose, Sabrina thought, that Deborah's wish to be alone with her father was not prompted by a desire for some romantic moments but part of a plan to persuade him to send her away to that rehabilitation home? Rehabilitation — the word always made her feel like a criminal.

'Please, God,' Sabrina prayed, 'don't let Daddy listen to her. I don't want to go to that place. Surely there must be an alternative besides another school.'

She felt guilty praying to God for help. It hurt to need anyone to help her. She had always been so completely self-sufficient. Now she was constantly depending on someone. At this very minute, Deborah might be persuading her father to send her to another school and she was sitting in the car, accepting her fate by the very fact that she was not participating in the discussion but calling on someone else to intercede on her behalf.

Thousands of times Sabrina had walked from the parking lot of the harbor to the slip where her father tied his boat. It wasn't that great a distance. If she remained calm and took her time, there was no reason why she couldn't traverse it again.

Artistically long fingers tightened the cord of the striped tunic and adjusted the rolled collar of the navy dark turtleneck she wore underneath. The wind whistled a warning outside. She ran a smoothing hand up to the back of her head to be certain her mink-brown hair was securely fastened in its knot atop her head.

Taking a deep breath to still the quivering excitement racing through her, Sabrina opened the door and swung her long legs on to the pavement. With the car door closed behind her and the cane firmly in her grasp, she moved slowly in the direction of the harbor fence. The icy tendrils of fear dancing down her spine added to the adventurous thrill of her small journey.

Emboldened by her initial success, Sabrina unconsciously began to hurry. She stumbled over a concrete parking stop and couldn't regain her balance. The cane slipped from her hand, skittering away as she sprawled on to the pavement.

Excitement disappeared immediately, leaving only black fear. Her shaking fingers reached for the cane, but it was out of her grasp. Except for the shock to her senses, there was no pain. She wasn't hurt, but how was she going to make her way to the dock without the cane?

'Damn, damn, damn!' Sabrina cursed her own foolishness for making the attempt in the first place.

If her father found her like this, it would only increase the apparent validity of Deborah's argument that Sabrina needed more professional help. Propping herself up on one elbow, she tried to check the rising terror that was leading her toward panic and think her way out of this predicament rationally.

'Are you all right?' The low, masculine voice offering concern was laced with amusement.

Sabrina's head jerked in the direction from which it had come, embarrassed red surging into her cheeks that a stranger should find her and humiliation that she was forced to seek his help.

The triangular line of her chin, tapering from prominent cheekbones and square jaw, tilted to a proud angle. 'I'm not hurt,' she asserted quickly, then grudgingly, 'My cane, would you get it for me?'

'Of course.' The amusement disappeared.

The instant the cane was retrieved Sabrina reached out to take it from him, not wanting to endure the mortification of his pity and hoping a quick 'thank you' would send him on his way. As her outstretched hand remained empty, her cheeks flamed darker.

A pair of strong hands slipped under her arms and bodily lifted her to her feet before she could gasp a protest. Her fingers touched the hard flesh of his upper arms, covered by the smooth material of his windbreaker. The salty tang of the ocean breeze mingled with the spicy after-shave cologne and his virile masculine scent. Sabrina was tall, nearly five foot seven, but the warm breath from his mouth stirred the bangs covering her wide forehead, making him easily six inches taller than she.

Her cane, hooked over his arm, tapped the side of her leg. 'Please let me go,' she said crisply while her fingers closed over the cane and lifted it from his arm.

'Nothing sprained but your pride, is that it?' the man mocked gently, loosening his grip on her slim waist and letting his hands fall away.

Sabrina smiled tautly, keeping her luminous brown eyes, that sometimes seemed too large for her face, averted from the man's face. His pity she didn't need.

'Thank you for your help,' she murmured unwillingly as she took a hesitant step backward.

Turning away, she waited for interminable seconds for him to continue wherever it was that he was going. She could feel his eyes on her back and guessed that he was waiting to be certain she hadn't hidden an injury from the fall.

Afraid that he might feel compelled because of her need for the cane to offer further assistance, Sabrina stepped out boldly. The shocking blare of a horn simultaneously accompanied by the squeal of car brakes paralyzed her. A steel band circled her waist and roughly pulled her back.

The husky male voice was still low, but there was nothing gentle and concerned about its tone as he growled in her ear. 'Were you trying to kill yourself? Didn't you see that car coming?'

'How could I?' Sabrina muttered bitterly, unable to tug the steel-hard arm from around her waist. 'I'm blind!'

She heard and felt his swift intake of breath a split second before he spun her around, her upper arms now prisoners of his hands. His eyes burned over her face. Her downcast chin was seized by his fingers and jerked up. Sabrina knew her sightless eyes were gazing into his face. For once she was blessedly glad she couldn't see. The pity that would be in his expression would have been unbearable.

'Why the hell didn't you say so!' There was a savage snap to his angry voice that caught her off guard. Anger she had not expected. 'And why the blazes isn't your cane white?'

Stung, Sabrina retorted in kind. 'Why am I supposed to have a white cane? Why am I expected to wear dark glasses? Should I run around with a little tin cup, too, crying "alms for the blind"? Why does being blind make me different from anyone else? Why do I have to be singled out? I hate it when parents point their fingers at me and tell their children to let the blind lady go first. My cane isn't white because I don't want any special consideration or any pity!'

'And your abhorrence of white canes nearly got you killed,' the stranger said grimly. 'Had the driver of the car that almost ran you down seen a white cane in your hand, he might have taken extra precautions, slowed down to give you the right of way or perhaps honked his horn to be sure you knew he was there. You go right on being a proud fool. You won't live long. Just keep on stepping in front of cars and sooner or later one of them will hit you. It might not trouble your conscience, but I'm sure the driver who ultimately runs you down will have difficulty understanding the pride that kept you from carrying a white cane that could have saved your life.'

'It's not difficult to understand,' Sabrina replied in a strangled voice. 'If the man had ever lost his sight, he'd know how grating it is to advertise your blindness.'

'It's very obvious why you reject pity from others,' the man taunted. 'You're much too busy wallowing in a pool of your own self-pity.'

'Of all the arrogant —' Sabrina didn't bother to finish the statement as her hand accurately judged the distance and height before connecting with a resounding slap against the man's jaw and cheek.

The trajectory of her hand had not completed its arc when she felt a stinging hand against her own cheek. It was no more than a reproving tap, but her shock at his reaction magnified it tenfold.

'How dare you strike a blind person!' she exclaimed in an outraged whisper.

'I thought you didn't want any special privileges?' he mocked. 'Or doesn't that extend to slapping another person, secure in the belief that he wouldn't retaliate against a blind girl? You'll have to make up your mind whether the kid gloves should be on or off.'

Sabrina gasped sharply, caught in the trap of her own words. 'You are insufferable!' she breathed, and turned away.

'Not so fast.' The hand digging into her shoulder and neck effectively halted her steps. 'You're worse than a toddler,' he muttered impatiently. 'Do you hear any cars coming? Do you know where you're going? Have you got your directions straight?'

'Just leave me alone!' Sabrina demanded. 'My well-being is nobody's responsibility but my own!'

'I'm sorry.' There was no apology in his harsh tone. 'But I was raised to believe that all of us are our brother's keeper, or sister's as the case may be. So, whether you like it or not, I'm going to see that you safely arrive at whatever destination you have. Go ahead and walk away.' Sabrina could sense his shrug of indifference. 'I'll be walking right behind you.'

She wanted to scream her frustration, but the stranger's unrelenting manner seemed to say that even that would be a waste of energy. She could not go on the docks, not with this man as an unwanted body-guard. The last thing she wanted was to have her father feel that it wasn't safe to leave her alone even for a few minutes. The minute her father saw this man at her side there would be all sorts of questions and the entire embarrassing story would be told.

Reluctantly she turned back in the direction she had just come. 'You don't need to trouble yourself,' she said stiffly. 'I'm only going to the car.'

'And drive, I suppose.' Satirical amusement was back in the man's low-pitched voice.

Sabrina chose to ignore his laughing jibe. Embarrassment and anger had all but erased her sense of humor. She tried to step past the tall stranger, but he moved to block her way.

'Which car?' he asked softly.

'The blue Continental behind you in the next row.'

'That isn't where you were headed when I first saw you.'

She gritted her teeth. 'I had intended to go out on the docks to meet my father and Deborah. Since you insist on accompanying me, I prefer to wait for them in the car.' There was a saccharine quality to her carefully enunciated words.

'They're out sailing and left you here in the car?' His tone seemed to indicate that her father and Deborah possessed as little sense as she did.

'No, my father went sailing. Deborah and I came down to pick him up. She's somewhere out on the dock now and I was going to see what was keeping them,' Sabrina retorted.

'Deborah is your sister?'

'You seem determined to pry into my personal life,' she sighed impatiently. 'Deborah will quite likely be my new mother — if it's any of your business!'

His hand closed over her elbow, the firm hold guiding her steps in the direction Sabrina knew the car to be. Several steps later, the end of the cane clunked against the side fender of the car.

'Which slip does your father use? I'll go see what's keeping him for you,' the man offered.

'No, thank you,' she refused curtly. 'He's nearly convinced already that I need a permanent baby-sitter. If you go carrying tales to him, I'll never be able to persuade him that I don't want anybody wiping my nose for me.' Exasperation ringed her voice. 'If I give you my word that I won't leave the car, will you go away and leave me alone?'

'I'm afraid it's too late to keep our meeting a secret from your father,' the man said.

'What do you mean?' Sabrina frowned.

'Is Deborah a redhead?'

'Yes.'

'Well, there's a man walking toward the harbor gates with a redhead at his side. He's looking this way with a rather anxious frown on his face,' was the reply.

'Please go quickly before he gets here,' she pleaded.

'Since he's already seen me, if I were your father I would be very suspicious if a strange man was talking to my daughter and left when he saw me coming. It's better that I stay,' the man stated.

'No.' Sabrina whispered her protest. With this man, words held little persuasion.

There was the clink of the harbor fence gates opening and closing. Time had run out.

'Stop looking as if I'd made some indecent proposition to you. Smile.' The sound of the man's low voice held a smile, warm and faintly amused at her apparent discomfort. Her reluctance was obvious as the corners of her mouth stretched into a slow smile.

'Sabrina.' Her father's voice hailed her, an undertone of concern in his otherwise warmly happy use of her name. 'Were you getting tired of waiting?'

Nervously she turned, trying to keep the faltering smile in place, knowing how perceptively discerning the scrutiny of his hazel eyes could be.

'Hello, Dad.' She forced a casualness into her voice. 'Did you have a good sail?'

'What else?' he laughed his assertion.

Sabrina sensed almost the exact instant when her father's inquisitive gaze was turned on the man at her side. She had been so busy trying to get rid of him that she hadn't thought of a single excuse to explain his presence.

The problem was taken out of her hands. 'You must be Sabrina's father. She was just asking me if I'd seen the *Lady Sabrina* come in while I was at the docks. I have the ketch down the way from yours, *Dame Fortune*. The name is Bay Cameron,' the stranger introduced.

'Grant Lane,' her father countered, the vague wariness leaving his voice at the introduction.

Unconsciously Sabrina had been holding her breath. She let it out in a silent sigh. The stranger, now identified as Bay Cameron, could think on his feet, she decided with relief. Of course she was certain there wasn't another boat in the harbor named *Lady Sabrina*, but the man had been quick to put two and two together simply from her father's use of her name. And it sounded like such a plausible excuse for her to be talking to him.

Her father's hand touched her shoulder and she turned her face to him with an easy smile. 'You weren't worrying about me, were you, Sabrina?' he teased.

'Not a bit. Not a salty old sailor like you. Of course, you were minus the best deckhand you ever had,' she laughed.

'Yes, well —' His stumbling agreement made Sabrina wish she could bite off her tongue. She had not meant to remind him of the many hours they had spent together sailing these very same waters before the accident that had left her permanently blind.

'Women always worry when their men are at sea,' the stranger named Bay Cameron filled in the awkward gap.

'It's our nature,' Deborah spoke up in her best purring voice. 'You men wouldn't like it any other way.'

'Quite right, Deborah,' her father agreed. 'Mr. Cameron, this is my fiancée, Deborah Mosely.'

'Miss Mosely, it's a pleasure, but I shouldn't keep you any longer. I'm sure you all have plans of some kind,' Bay Cameron responded.

'Thank you for keeping Sabrina company.' There was sincere gratitude in her father's offer of thanks.

'Yes, Mr. Cameron,' Sabrina added, reluctantly acknowledging the fact that he had not given her away. 'I appreciated your thoughtfulness.'

'Yes, I know.' Lack of sight made Sabrina's hearing more acute. She caught the mocking inflection in his words that quite likely escaped her father and Deborah's ears. He knew very well what she was thanking him for. 'Perhaps we'll all see each other again some time. Good afternoon.'

After their answering chorus of goodbyes, Sabrina listened to his footsteps fading away to another area of the parking lot. She wondered why he had not seen fit, in his arrogance, to tell her father the way they had really met. Pity, most likely, although he had certainly exhibited a remarkable lack of it earlier. In fact he had been downright rude and tyrannical.

The car door was opened behind her, bringing an abrupt end to her wandering thoughts as her father's guiding hand helped her into the back seat.

'I thought you were going to wait in the car,' Deborah said in a faintly reproving tone after they were all seated.

'It got stuffy, so I decided to get some fresh air,' Sabrina lied.

'It did put some color in your cheeks,' Grant Lane observed. 'You probably should get out more.'

Was that an innocent comment or a remark prompted by a discussion with Deborah concerning that new school for the blind she had heard about? It was impossible to tell. Sabrina crossed her fingers.

'This Mr. Cameron,' Deborah said, 'had you met him before?'

'No. Why?' Sabrina stiffened, vaguely on the defensive.

'It's not like you to talk to total strangers, that's all,' the redhead replied.

'You mean, not since I've been blind,' Sabrina corrected sharply. 'I've never been exactly shy. Besides, all I did was ask about Dad.'

There was a moment of uneasy silence. Her reply hadn't needed to be so cutting, but sometimes Deborah's air of solicitude and apparent concern got on Sabrina's nerves. For that matter, anyone's did.

'Do you suppose,' Deborah covered the silence, 'he's one of the real estate Camerons?'

'I can't visualize any other having a ketch in the Yacht Harbor,' her father replied. 'The Camerons are one of the founding families of San Francisco.'

A native San Franciscan, Sabrina was well aware of the city's colorful history. Until gold was discovered in 1849, it had been a nothing little settlement on San Francisco Bay called Yerba Buena, 'good herb.' The bay was a perfect harbor for the ships racing around the tip of South America to join in the rush for California gold. The natural entrance into the bay truly became 'golden gates' for a lot of pioneers.

Few actually found the precious metal in any quantity, but the real treasure had been in the goods and services they brought with them. The great bulk of the gold was possessed by a very small number of men. The majority of it from the California and Nevada lodes built San Francisco, the City by the Bay.

The Cameron family was one of the less publicized of the original founders. It was laughingly said that they once owned all of San Francisco, and now they possessed only a quarter of the city. Hardly a step down in this day and age, Sabrina thought wryly, and it certainly accounted for the man's arrogance.

Oh, well, she sighed, what was the use in thinking about him? He was not the kind of man a person would run into very often, not with his background.

She had rather liked his voice, though. Sabrina qualified the thought quickly. She had liked it when he hadn't been dictatorially telling her what to do. The low baritone pitch had been warm and vaguely caressive, mature, too. She wondered how old he was.

That was one of the problems of not being able to see. She had to rely so heavily on the other senses to judge the new people she met. Still, she was becoming rather good at it. She began a quick exercise of the impressions she had gained in her brief meeting with Bay Cameron.

He was tall, over six foot by at least an inch. When he had pulled her out of the oncoming car's path, she had had the sensation of wide shoulders, a flat stomach and lean hips. Judging by the solidness of his muscles he was in excellent physical condition. The salty ocean spray that had clung to him at least verified that he often journeyed forth in the ketch tied up in the harbor and probably had that day since the scent had been predominant. That indicated an affection for the sea or at least the outdoors, possibly both. His clean male scent and the fragrantly spicy after-shave cologne told her a bit about his personal habits.

At the time she had been too angry to appreciate his sense of humor, but she guessed it was there, somewhere beneath his amused mockery. His intelligence was in some ways measured by his educated manner of speaking and the quick thinking that had immediately assimilated the facts and come up with a reasonable excuse for her father as to why Sabrina had been talking to him. On the business side, he would probably be very shrewd and astute. The family fortune would be safe with him, if not increased.

She settled back into her seat with smug triumph. That was a great deal of information to glean from one meeting. There were only two things about him she didn't know. His age she could only narrow as being somewhere between thirty and fifty, judging by the maturity of his voice and his physical condition. The second was a detailed description of his looks — the color of his hair, his eyes, that type of thing. Sabrina was really quite pleased with herself.

For an instant she was motionless. There was one other thing she didn't know — his marital status. That was something she couldn't be certain of even if she could see, unless he was one of those men who faithfully wore his wedding ring. She couldn't recall the sensation of anything metal on his fingers.

Not that she cared one way or the other whether he was married or not. She had merely been conducting an exercise of her senses, a satisfactory one at that.

Two

Sabrina licked the vanilla icing from her fingers, then painstakingly ran the knife across the top of every centimeter of the cake. No matter what kind of cake she made, her father invariably called it a fingerprint cake. Sabrina was never totally confident that the frosting covered the entire cake. The only way she could be certain was by feeling, hence the telltale impressions of her fingers across the icing.

Placing the knife on the Formica counter, she set the cake platter toward the back, refusing to give in to the sensation that there was a gaping hole somewhere exposing the dark devil's food cake. Before the accident that had left her blinded, Sabrina had taken the simplest task in the kitchen for granted.

Now, washing dishes was a study in diligence, let alone cooking a meal. She had mastered nearly everything but eggs. There was only one type she could cook. Invariably they turned out to be scrambled omelettes. For the sake of their stomachs, breakfast had become the meal her father prepared.

Sunday was the day that Deborah did all the cooking, as had been the case this last weekend. She was a gourmet cook. Sabrina had always been mediocre at best, which made her doubly conscious of the occasionally charred or rare meals she placed on the table during the week compared to the perfection of Deborah's. Yet her father had never complained once, ignoring the less appetizing to compliment the good.

Except for a daily woman who came in twice a week to do the more thorough cleaning, Sabrina took care of the house herself, dusting and vacuuming. It took her longer than the average sighted person, but she had discovered that, with patience, there was very little she couldn't do. But patience was the key.

Without the benefit of sunlight, the passage of time was nearly impossible to judge. It seemed to slip through her fingers at times, five minutes turning out to be ten. Sometimes when the loneliness of her dark world caved in about her, the opposite was true. The empty, desolate sensation invariably occurred after a great surge of creative energy that she was unable to release.

Sabrina had learned to endure the myriad inconveniences that came from being sightless. She could even keep the bitterness in check until she thought about the career that had come to such an abrupt halt after the accident.

Since almost the first time a watercolor brush had been put in her hand, art and more specifically painting had been her special love. Her natural talent, enhanced by skill taught by some of the best teachers around, had made her a relatively successful artist at the early age of twenty-two, thanks to nearly fifteen years of training. Recognition had been achieved in portraits, not necessarily commissioned sittings but more often interesting faces she had seen along Fisherman's Wharf or Little Italy.

That had been the cruelty in the accident that had taken her sight. It had been a car accident. Even to this day Sabrina didn't know what had happened. She had been driving home very late at night after a weekend spent with a girl friend in Sacramento. She had fallen asleep at the wheel.

Looking back, her haste to return home seemed so senseless, considering the month she had spent in the hospital recovering from broken ribs and a concussion — not to mention the evident blow to her head that had irreparably damaged the optic nerves.

Giving her head a firm shake, Sabrina resolutely tried to push such memories to the back of her mind. Her survival lay in the future, not in looking over her shoulder at the past. At the moment the future looked empty, but seven months ago Sabrina had not believed she would accomplish as much as she had.

Her next obstacle was walking from her home to the drugstore to buy a bottle of shampoo. It was only five blocks, but it was five blocks of San Francisco traffic and four intersections. Only in the last two months had she had sufficient confidence in her ability to attempt such a journey without accompaniment. Her pride always kept the humiliation of getting lost uppermost in her mind.

The pale green sweater jacket Sabrina took from the closet complemented the dark green of her slacks. She touched the handle of her oak cane in the umbrella stand, the smooth finish of the wood reminding her instantly of the arrogant stranger Bay Cameron that she had met at the Yacht Harbor last Sunday. She didn't care what he thought. She preferred the anonymity of a wooden cane. It was bad enough blundering about in her permanent darkness without drawing attention to her plight.

Entering into the stairway, Sabrina walked down the steps to the front door, carefully locking it behind her. The grillework gates just a few feet away creaked noisily as she opened and locked them. The sidewalk sloped abruptly downward. Sabrina counted the paces slowly, accurately turning at the front door of the neighboring Victorian house.

Pressing the intercom buzzer, she waited for her neighbor's response. As a precaution, her father insisted that she always let someone know where she was going and when she had safely returned, whether it was Peggy Collins, their neighbor for nearly fifteen years, or himself at his office.

'Yes, who is it?' a briskly sharp female voice answered the buzz.

'It's me, Sabrina. I'm on my way to the drugstore. Do you need anything?'

'How about three more hands? Or better yet, a plane ticket to South America?' the woman replied with amused exasperation.

'It's as bad as that, is it?' Sabrina laughed.

'Ken called me an hour ago and is bringing a couple of very important clients home for cocktails and dinner. Naturally there's not a thing in the house to eat and I'm also defrosting the refrigerator and have the contents of half the closets strewn through the house. It looks as if a cyclone had hit this place. Of all days to get ambitious, I had to pick today.'

'I'll be back in an hour or so.' Sabrina smiled at the intercom. There always seemed to be an impending crisis at Peggy's house that was invariably weathered with commendable aplomb. 'If we have anything you need — ice, drink, food — you just let me know.'

'My best solution is to find a husband with a better sense of timing,' Peggy sighed. 'Take care, Sabrina. I'll let you know if I need anything when you get back.'

Humming softly, Sabrina started out again. Her neighbor's droll humor had restored her somewhat dampened spirits. The trip to the drugstore became more of an adventure than an obstacle. There was a nip in the wind racing down the hill, but there always seemed to be a nip in the winds wandering through San Francisco.

There was no warmth on her cheeks as she crossed to the normally more sunny side of the street. The sun had evidently not burned through the fog yet. Instantly a vision of the fog swirling about the spans of the Golden Gate bridge sprang to her mind.

Her concentration broke for a moment and she had to pause to get her bearings. It was so difficult not to daydream. The end of her cane found the drop box for the mail and she knew which block she was on.

Crossing the street, she began counting her steps. She didn't want to walk into the barbershop instead of the drugstore as she had done the last time. A funny, prickly sensation started down the back of her neck. She ran a curious finger along the back collar of her sweater jacket and frowned at the unknown cause of the peculiar feeling.

'No white cane, I see,' a familiarly husky voice said from behind her. 'You're a stubborn girl, Miss Lane.'

A disbelieving paralysis took hold of her limbs for a fleeting second before Sabrina pivoted toward the male voice.

'Mr. Cameron,' she acknowledged him coolly. 'I didn't expect to see you again.'

'The city isn't as large as it seems. Here I am driving down the street and see a girl walking with a cane. I start wondering if you've been run down yet. Then, lo and behold, I realize the young girl with the cane is you. Are you in search of your father again?' Bay Cameron asked in that faintly amused tone she remembered.

'I was just going into the drugstore here.' Sabrina motioned absently over her shoulder in the general direction of her destination. 'You were driving?'

'Yes, I parked my car up the street. Do you live near here?'

'A few blocks,' she answered, tilting her head curiously and wishing she could see the expression on his face. 'Why did you stop?'

'To see if you would have a cup of coffee with me,' he replied smoothly.

'Why?' She couldn't keep the wariness out of her voice.

Bay Cameron laughed softly. 'Do I have to have an ulterior motive? Why can't it just be a friendly gesture on my part?'

'I just don't understand why you should want to have coffee with —' Sabrina nearly said 'with a blind girl'. The haughtiness left her voice as she ended lamely with '— me.'

'It seems to me, Sabrina, that you not only suffer from a persecution complex but a feeling of inferiority as well,' he suggested mockingly.

'That's absurd!' The sightless brown eyes that had been directed blankly at his face were sharply averted to the traffic in the street.

'Good.' Strong fingers closed over her elbow, turning her toward the drugstore. 'Where would you like to have the coffee? I know a little cafe in the next block we could go to.'

'I'm sure your wife would much prefer you spend your free time with her.' She made another feeble protest.

'I'm sure she would — if I had a wife.'

'I — I have an errand in the drugstore,' Sabrina protested again.

'Will it take long?'

Hopelessly she wished it would take an hour. She was simply reluctant to spend any time with him. That air of confidence that surrounded him did make her feel inferior.

'No,' she admitted with a downcast chin, 'it shouldn't take very long.'

'Your lack of enthusiasm isn't very flattering,' Bay Cameron taunted softly. 'Would you feel more comfortable if I waited outside for you?'

Just knowing he was in the vicinity unnerved her. Sabrina shook her head. 'It doesn't make any difference.'

'In that case, I'll go in with you. I need some cigarettes.'

She felt the brush of his arm against her shoulder as he reached around her to open the door. Her elbow was released and she entered the store more or less on her own. She tapped her way to the rear counter, sighing as she heard Bay Cameron's footsteps heading toward the tobacco section.

'Is there something I can help you find?' a woman clerk's voice asked.

Before Sabrina could reply, another gruffly happy voice broke in, male this time. 'Sabrina, I was beginning to think you had forgotten where my store was. I have not seen you in nearly two weeks.'

'Hello, Gino.' She smiled widely in the direction of the reproachful voice.

16

'It is all right, Maria, I will help Sabrina. You go see what that man at the prescription counter wants,' he dismissed the clerk that had initially approached Sabrina. As the woman's footsteps moved away, Gino Marchetti whispered, 'Maria is new, a cousin of my wife's sister's husband. This is only her first week, so she doesn't know my regular customers.'

Those who worked in Gino's drugstore pharmacy were always related to him in some way, Sabrina had learned over the years. But she knew the information had been offered to gently apologize for the woman not knowing Sabrina was blind.

'She has a very nice voice. I'm sure she'll soon learn,' she replied.

'What is it that you need this day? Name it and I will get it for you.'

'Some shampoo.' Sabrina gave him the brand name she wanted.

While he went to get it, she carefully felt through the paper money in her wallet, marked by a certain fold to distinguish the denominations, for the amount she owed him.

As he was ringing up the sale on his old cash register, Gino Marchetti said, 'I still have the picture you painted of me hanging on this wall. People come in all the time and say, 'That looks just like you' and I say, 'Of course, it is me.' I tell them that the girl who painted it has come to my store since she was a little thing and that you painted it from memory and gave it to me on the anniversary of my twenty-fifth year in business. Everyone thinks it is a very fine gift to have.'

'I'm glad you like it, Gino,' Sabrina smiled wanly.

She remembered vividly how proud he had been that day she had presented the portrait to him nearly two years ago. It was that ever-present aura of pride that she had tried to capture in his likeness. It was a loving, generous pride and she had been relatively satisfied with the result. Now she would never know that sense of creative accomplishment again.

'Sabrina, I didn't mean —'

She heard the hint of regret and self-reproach in the elderly Italian's voice and guessed that some of her sadness had tugged down the corners of her mouth. She determinedly curved it upward again and interrupted him.

'It was really a very small gift, Gino,' deliberately misinterpreting the statement of apology he had been about to make. 'The painting

17

was just a small way of saying thank you for all those peppermint sticks you gave me.'

The sensation of being watched tingled down her neck. Sabrina wasn't surprised when Bay Cameron spoke. Her sensitive radar seemed to be tuned to his presence.

'You did this painting?' he asked quietly.

'Yes.' She snipped off the end of the affirmation.

'It is very good, isn't it?' Gino prompted. 'I sold Sabrina her very first crayons. Then it was watercolors, then colored chalk. In my small way I helped her to become an artist, and she gave me this portrait as a present. She always comes to my store once, sometimes twice a week. That is, until her accident,' his voice became sad. 'Now she doesn't come as often.' Sabrina moved uneasily and Gino's mood immediately changed to a gayer note. 'Last week I saw her walk by my store and I wonder to myself where she is going. Then I see her walk into the barbershop next door and I say to myself 'Oh no, she is going to have that beautiful crown of hair on top of her head cut off, but she had only walked into the wrong store. She was coming to see me.'

'Do you know the very first time I saw her and that little knot of silky brown hair on top of her head, it reminded me of a crown, too.' There was a caressive quality to Bay Cameron's softly musing voice. Sabrina felt the rise of pink in her cheeks.

'I've taken up enough of your time, Gino,' she said hastily. 'I know you have work to do and other customers waiting. I'll see you next week.'

'Be sure it is next week, Sabrina.'

'I will. *Ciao*, Gino.' She turned quickly, aware of Bay Cameron stepping out of her way and following, although there was no guiding hand at her elbow.

'*Addio*, Sabrina,' Gino responded, not showing the least surprise that the stranger was with her.

'The cafe is to the left,' Bay instructed her as they walked out of the store. 'It's around the corner and down a short flight of stairs.'

'I think I know which one you mean. I haven't been there in several years,' Sabrina said stiffly.

They walked side by side down the sidewalk to the corner. He made no attempt to guide her, letting her make her own way without any assistance.

'That was a very good painting,' Bay ended the silence. 'Did you have training as a child?'

'I took lessons nearly all my life.' She swallowed the lump in her throat and replied calmly. 'It was my career. I was relatively successful.'

'I can believe it,' he agreed. 'You were good.'

'"Were" being the operative word,' she inserted with faint bitterness. Then she took a shaky breath. 'I'm sorry.'

'Don't apologize,' he seemed to shrug. 'It must have been a doubly cruel blow as an artist to lose your sight. There's bound to be a feeling of injustice, otherwise you wouldn't be human.' There was a light touch on her arm to attract her attention. 'The iron banister of the stairs is on your left. You can follow it to the stairwell,' he instructed.

When her left hand encountered the railing, his own hand returned to his side. He had accepted the pain she felt at the loss of her career as a natural thing, hardly needing an explanation. There had been no empty words as others had offered that some day she would get over it. That Sabrina had never been able to believe.

At the base of the stairs, Bay reached past her to open the cafe door. A hand rested firmly on the side of her waist and remained there as a hostess showed them to a small booth.

'Let me take your cane,' he offered. 'I'll hang it on the post beside your seat so it will be out of the way.'

Sabrina handed it to him and slid into the booth, her fingers resting nervously on the table top. In the past she had avoided public eating establishments, too self-conscious to be at ease. She touched the edge of a menu and pushed it aside.

Their waitress had evidently appeared at the table because she heard Bay ask for two coffees before he addressed a question to her. 'They make their own pastries here. They're very good. Would you like any, Sabrina?'

'No.' In her nervousness she was too abrupt and she quickly added, 'No, thank you.'

'Would you like a cigarette?' he offered.

'Please.' She accepted almost with a sigh of relief.

The waitress arrived with their coffee just as Bay placed a lit cigarette between her fingers and slid the ashtray in front of her discreetly searching hand. Sabrina drew deeply on the filter tip of the cigarette, slightly amazed that she could feel the warmth of his mouth on the cigarette.

'Do you take anything in your coffee?' Bay asked.

'Nothing, thank you.' Sabrina exhaled the smoke from her mouth, blowing away some of her tension at the same time.

The heat from the coffee made the cup easy to find. The fingers of one hand closed around its warmth. A silence followed, one that Sabrina was pleasantly surprised to discover as comfortable. Her first meeting with Bay Cameron had been tainted by his apparent arrogance. It still existed, proved by the very fact that he had maneuvered her into this cafe, but it had somehow been tempered by his understanding.

In spite of that disturbing argument about the white cane, he seemed to approve of her desire for independence. The assistance he had given her had been unobtrusive. That coupled with his matter-of-fact comment about her loss of career made Sabrina wonder if she shouldn't re-assess her opinion of him. Bay Cameron seemed to be an unusual man. Sabrina wished she had met him before she lost her sight. He might have made an interesting portrait study. Then she sighed.

'What was that for?' he chided mockingly.

'Wishing,' Sabrina shrugged.

'A common pastime?'

'Only when I have nothing to distract me. Sometimes,' she ran a finger around the rim of her cup, 'I wonder when I'm alone if I wasn't given the gift of seeing people, places and things in minute detail early in life so I could store up a treasure of beautiful scenes to remember.'

'Do you believe in fate, then?' Bay asked quietly.

'Sometimes it seems the only explanation. Do you?' Sabrina countered.

'I believe we were given certain talents and abilities. What we do with them is the mark of our own character. I can't accept that I might not be the master of my own destiny.' His reply was laced with self-directed humor.

'I doubt there's very little you've wanted that you haven't obtained,' she agreed with a faint smile.

'Perhaps. And perhaps I've just been careful about what I wanted.' The smile faded from his voice. 'Tell me, Sabrina, how long has it been since you lost your sight?'

She was beginning to learn that Bay Cameron had a habit of coming straight to the point. Most of the people she knew or had met took special care to avoid any reference to her blindness and took pains that the conversation didn't contain words that referred to sight.

'Almost eight months.' She inhaled the smoke from the cigarette, wondering why his frankness didn't disconcert her. Maybe it was because he didn't seem embarrassed or self-conscious about her blindness.

'No days or hours?' There was the impression of a brow raised mockingly in her direction.

'I stopped trying to keep an exact count after the fourth specialist told my father and me that I would never see again.' Sabrina tried to sound nonchalant, but there was a faint catch to her voice.

'What happened?'

'A car crash. It was late at night. I was driving home from Sacramento and fell asleep at the wheel. I don't know what happened.' Her fingers fluttered uncertainly in the air, then returned to grip the coffee cup. 'I came to in a hospital. There weren't any witnesses. A passing motorist saw my wrecked car in the ditch, the authorities estimate several hours after the accident.'

Sabrina waited for the supposedly bolstering comments that usually followed when she related the details of the accident, the it-could-have-been-worse and the you're-lucky-you-weren't-paralyzed-or-maimed sentences. But none of those trite words were spoken.

'What are you going to do now?'

'I don't know.' She didn't have the answer to that problem. She took a sip of her coffee. 'I've just been taking one day at a time, learning over again how to do all the things I used to take for granted. I was so positive that I was going to have a career in art that I never studied anything else but reading, writing and arithmetic. I'm going to have to make a decision about my future pretty soon, though,' she sighed. 'I can't keep being a burden for my father.'

'I doubt if he thinks of you that way.'

'I know *he* doesn't.' Unconsciously she put qualifying emphasis on the masculine pronoun.

Bay Cameron was much too observant to miss it. 'But someone else does, is that it?' he questioned. 'Is it your father's fiancée?'

Sabrina opened her mouth to deny it, then nodded reluctantly that he was right. 'I don't blame Deborah. She wants Dad to herself —' She hesitated. 'I don't want you to misunderstand me. I do like her. As a matter of fact, I'm the one who introduced her to him. She has a small antique shop here in San Francisco. It's just that we both know it would never work for the two of us to live in the same house. She wants me to go to some school she heard about where blind people are taught new skills, not basket-weaving or anything as humbling as that, but legitimate skills. They have a job placement program, too, when you've completed the term.'

'What does your father think of the idea?'

'I don't believe she's mentioned it to him yet.' A wry smile pulled her mouth into a crooked line. 'I think she wants to weigh me down with guilt so I'll be in favor of it when Dad brings up the subject.'

'Do you feel guilty?' Bay asked as she carefully stubbed out her cigarette in the ashtray.

'I suppose so. It's only natural, isn't it?' Sabrina spread out the fingers of her hands on the table top, looking at them as if she could see them. 'Everyone wants to think of himself as useful.'

'And you don't do anything that you consider useful?'

'I take care of the house and do most of the cooking. I could hardly keep doing that after Dad and Deborah are married. After all, it would be her house then.' She continued staring sightlessly at her long fingers. 'I know I could learn something.' She shook her head wearily, closing her hands around the coffee cup again. 'I'm still filled with too much pride, too much self-importance. My hands have always held an artist's brush. I guess it's just a case of not wanting to let go of that. Which is probably why I keep putting off the day when they'll have to do something else.'

'What does your boyfriend say to all this?'

'Boyfriend? I haven't got a boyfriend. A lot of men who are friends, but no boyfriends,' Sabrina denied firmly.

'You're a very attractive girl. I find it hard to believe that you didn't have a romantic attachment for someone,' Bay commented in a doubting voice.

'I always had my career,' she shrugged. 'I dated, quite often, as a matter of fact. I simply steered clear of any romantic involvement. Love and marriage were always something that would come somewhere in the future. I'm glad now that I did,' she added frankly. 'How many men would want to be saddled with a blind wife?'

'Isn't that a somewhat cynical view of the male sex?' he chuckled.

'Not really,' she smiled. 'It's not even a cynical view of love. It's just realistic. Being blind tends to make other people awkward and self-conscious. They're always trying to be so careful that they don't hurt your feelings by pointing out that there are some things blind people simply can't participate in, and that makes an uncomfortable relationship.'

'That's funny,' he mused mockingly. 'I don't feel the least bit uncomfortable, awkward or self-conscious, and I'm sitting here with you.'

For a moment, Sabrina was flustered by his observation. Mostly because it was true. There were no undercurrents of tension flowing around her.

'Actually I wasn't thinking about you,' she admitted. 'I was referring to some of my other friends, male and female. They all still keep in touch, the ones that count. They call or stop by to see me or invite me out, but it's not quite the same. With some of them our common link was art, so I understand why they don't like to bring up that subject in front of me. The others — there's just a vague uneasiness on both sides. With you,' Sabrina tilted her head to a curious angle, 'I don't really understand. I'm talking to you about things you couldn't possibly be interested in and I don't know why. Are you some kind of amateur psychiatrist?' A little frown of bewildered amusement puckered her brows.

'No.' Sabrina sensed his smile. 'And I wasn't at all bored. I imagine all of this has been building up inside you for some time. It's always easier to talk to strangers who don't have preconceived opinions. I happened to be an available stranger.'

'In that case, what wise advice do you have to offer me?' she asked with a pertly challenging smile.

'Strangers don't give advice. They only listen.' The laughter was obvious in his low voice as he dodged her question expertly.

Hurried footsteps approached their booth. 'Would you like some more coffee?' the waitress inquired.

'No more for me, thank you,' Sabrina refused. Her fingers touched the braille face of her watch, 'I have to be getting home.'

'Our check, please,' Bay requested.

By the time Sabrina had slid out of the booth seat, Bay was at her side, handing her the oak cane. His hand again rested lightly on the back of her waist, guiding her discreetly past the row of booths and tables to the cafe door. She waited there while he paid the check.

Once outside and up the stairs to the sidewalk, Bay asked, 'Did you say you only lived a few blocks from here?'

'Yes.' Sabrina turned her head toward him, the smile coming more easily and more often to her mouth. 'And it's uphill all the way.'

'Well, there's one consolation about the hills in San Francisco. When you get tired of walking up them, you can always lean against them.' Sabrina laughed at his amusingly accurate description. 'That's a nice sound,' Bay said lowly. 'I was beginning to think you'd lost the ability to laugh along with your sight. I'm glad you didn't.'

Her heart seemed to skip a beat for a few seconds. Sabrina discovered that she wanted to believe that was a personal comment and not a casual observation. That put her on dangerous ground, so she kept silent.

'My car is just around the corner,' Bay said as if he hadn't expected her to reply. 'Let me give you a ride home.'

It was past the hour Sabrina had told Peggy Collins she would be gone. That was why she agreed to his offer, giving him the address of the narrow Victorian house in the Pacific Heights section. The rush hour traffic had begun, so there was very little conversation between them in the car. Using the traffic at the intersections as a guide, Sabrina was able to judge when Bay turned on to the block where she lived.

'Our house is the dark gold one with the brown and white trim,' she told him. 'The number is difficult to see sometimes.'

A few seconds later, he was turning the wheels into the curb, setting the emergency brake and shutting off the motor. He had just walked around the car and opened her door when Sabrina heard her neighbor call out.

'Sabrina, are you all right?' The question was followed immediately by the sound of the redwood gate opening and Peggy Collins' footsteps hurrying toward them. 'I was just coming to see if you'd come home and forgotten to let me know.'

'I was longer than I expected to be,' Sabrina said, explaining the obvious.

'So I see.' The curious tone of voice also said that her neighbor saw the man Sabrina was with and was waiting to be introduced.

'Peggy, this is Bay Cameron. Peggy Collins is my neighbor,' she submitted to the invisible arm-twisting.

There was a polite exchange of greetings before Bay turned to Sabrina. 'It's my turn to say I'll have to be going, Sabrina.'

'Thank you for the coffee and the ride home.' She offered her hand to him in goodbye.

'My pleasure.' His grasp was warm and sure and all too brief. 'I'll see you again some time.'

The last sounded very much like a promise. Sabrina hoped that it was. His arrogance of their first meeting was completely erased. It was really strange how readily she had confided in him, she thought as she heard the car door open and close and the motor start. Not even to her father, who was very close to her, had Sabrina been able to talk that freely.

'Where did you meet him?' Peggy asked with more than idle curiosity.

'The other day at the Yacht Harbor when Deborah and I went to pick up Dad,' she explained, forgetting for an instant that her neighbor was standing beside her. 'I just bumped into him this afternoon — well, not literally,' Sabrina qualified. Her head followed the sound of the departing car until she could no longer hear it. She turned toward the older woman. 'Peggy, what does he look like?'

The woman paused, collecting her thoughts. 'He's tall, in his thirties I would say. He has reddish-brown hair and brown eyes, not dark brown but they are brown. I wouldn't call him handsome exactly. Good-looking isn't the right description either, although in a way they both fit.' There was another hesitation. 'He looks like a man. Do you know what I mean?'

'Yes,' Sabrina replied softly. 'Yes, I think I do,' guessing that his features were too strong and forceful to be classified in any other way.

'Good heavens!' Peggy exclaimed suddenly. 'I forgot to put the potatoes in the oven! I'll talk to you later, Sabrina.'

'Yes, all right, Peggy.' Her neighbor was already fast retreating to her door by the time Sabrina absently acknowledged her words.

Three

'Are you positive you want to walk out on the docks, Sabrina?' Deborah asked sharply.

'I would like to, yes,' she admitted. Unconsciously she raised her chin to a challenging angle. 'That is, of course, unless you want some time alone with Father.'

'It's not that,' the redhead sighed in frustration. 'Grant — worries about you so and there aren't any railings on the piers. He's naturally going to be concerned about your safety.'

'All parents worry, Deborah,' Sabrina said quietly. 'Father just feels he has more cause to worry than most, with justification, I suppose. I can't spend the rest of my life not doing things that might cause him to worry.'

'Believe me, if I could find a way to make him stop worrying about you, I would do it,' was Deborah's taut response as she stepped out of the car.

Sabrina followed, but more slowly, walking around the car parked in the lot of the Yacht Harbor to the side of her father's fiancée.

'Has Dad said any more about setting the date?' Sabrina asked as they started toward the fence gates.

'No, and I haven't brought up the subject.' There was a pause before Deborah continued. 'A long time ago I recognized the fact that I'm a jealous and possessive woman, Sabrina. If I married your father while you were still living at home, it would create friction among all of us. You would be hurt; your father would be hurt; and I would be hurt. I'm quite aware that you're a very independent person and have no desire to be a burden to your father for the rest of your life.'

'Which is why you're pushing the idea of this school,' Sabrina breathed in deeply, knowing the vast amount of truth in the red-head's words.

'It may not be the answer, Sabrina, but it is a start,' Deborah suggested earnestly.

'I need more time.' Sabrina lifted her chin into the wind, letting the light ocean breeze play over her face. 'I keep hoping there'll be some other alternative. I don't know what, but something.'

'You are considering the school, though?'

'I have to consider it,' she sighed, 'whether I like the idea or not.'

'Thank you.' Deborah's voice trembled slightly before it steadied with determination. 'I like you, Sabrina, but I love your father. I've waited a long time to meet a man like him. So please, understand why I'm pushing so hard to get you out of the house.'

'I do.' The wooden floor of the dock was beneath her feet, the harbor gate closed behind them. 'If I loved a man, I would be just as anxious as you to have him to myself. But I won't be rushed into a decision, not unless I'm sure there isn't anything else.'

Deborah's guiding hand claimed her elbow. 'Turn left here,' she instructed.

The titian-haired woman was aware of Sabrina's stubborn streak. This was the time to let the subject drop when she had achieved a minor capitulation that Sabrina would consider her suggestion.

Sabrina guessed her tactics and willingly changed the topic. 'Is Dad in?'

'Yes, he's tying everything down now,' was the reply. A few minutes later, Deborah called out, 'Hello, darling, did you have a good time?'

'Of course.' There was contented happiness in her father's voice that brought a smile to Sabrina's lips. 'Sabrina? I didn't expect to see you with Deborah.' A faint anxiety crept in.

'It was too nice a day to wait by the car.' She smiled away his concern. 'Don't worry, I'll be a good girl and not stray from the center of the dock.'

'I'll only be a few more minutes,' he promised.

'I'll get your thermos and things from the cabin, if you like, Grant,' Deborah offered.

There was hesitation before the suggestion was accepted. Sabrina knew her father was reluctant to leave her alone on the dock. His agreement was probably an indication that Deborah had given him a look that said he was being overly protective.

The creak of the boat was accompanied by the quiet lapping of the water against its hull. There was the flapping of wings near where Sabrina stood, followed by the cry of a gull. The ocean scent of salt and fish was in the breeze lifting the short hair on her forehead.

A tickling sensation teased the back of her neck. Instantly Sabrina was alert to the sounds of footsteps approaching, more than one set. Intuition said it was Bay Cameron and she knew all along that she had been hoping he would be there. But he was with someone, more than one, perhaps three others. The light tread of one pair of feet warned her that they belonged to a female.

'Are you calling it a day, Mr. Lane?' Bay Cameron's voice called out in greeting.

'Mr. Cameron, how are you?' her father returned with startled pleasure. 'Yes, this is all for me today until next week. Are you coming in or going out?'

'Out. We thought we'd take in an ocean sunset,' he replied, confirming that the other footsteps she had heard were with him. He had stopped beside her. Sabrina's radar told her he was only inches from her left side. 'How are you today, Sabrina?'

'Fine.' Her head bobbed self-consciously. She sensed the eagerness of the others to be on their way.

'I see you made it all the way on to the dock this time without mishap. Did you do it by yourself?' The words were spoken so soft and low that the light breeze couldn't carry them to anyone's ears but Sabrina's.

'No,' she murmured, barely moving her lips.

'Bay, are you coming?' an impatient female voice asked.

'Yes, Roni,' he answered. 'I'll see you again.' The ambiguous promise was offered as a goodbye. The raised pitch of his voice directed it to everyone and not Sabrina alone.

'Good sailing!' her father called out, but Sabrina said nothing.

A faint depression had settled in, intensified when the wind carried the woman's haughty inquiry as to who they were, but her acute hearing couldn't catch Bay's response.

Her fingers tightened around the curve of her oak cane. She was glad her cane was not white, identifying herself immediately to his friends as a blind girl. She could not have endured the sensation of their pitying looks. It was bad enough imagining the explanation Bay was giving them now. She wished she had not allowed him to bully her into having coffee with him the other day, never poured out her troubles to him with such a complete lack of discretion.

'Are you ready yet, Dad?' she asked sharply, suddenly anxious to be gone, finding no more enjoyment in the scent and the sounds of the sea.

'Be right there,' he answered. 'Have you got everything, Deborah?'

'Yes.'

Seconds later the two of them were at Sabrina's side, her father's arm curving around her shoulders and guiding her back the way she had come. For once she didn't try to shrug away his assistance. She wanted the protective comfort of his arm.

She had tried to block out the memory of that Sunday, but it remained a shadow lurking near the edges of her already dark world. The melancholy violin strains on the stereo were not easing her depression. The position of the furniture in their house had long been memorized, and she walked unerringly to the stereo and switched off the music.

The front door bell buzzed loudly into the ensuing silence. With an impatient sigh at the unwanted intrusion, Sabrina continued to the intercom that linked the street level entrance next to the garage with the living area of the house.

'Yes. Who is it?' she inquired briskly after her searching fingers had found the switch.

'Bay Cameron.'

A surprised stillness kept her silent for ticking seconds. There was no warmth in her voice when she asked. 'What is it you wanted, Mr. Cameron?'

'I'm not selling brushes, insurance or bibles,' his amused voice answered. 'The only reason I can think of why I might be standing in front of your door is to see you.'

'Why?'

'I never did like talking to boxes. Will you come down?'

Sabrina sighed in irritation at the challenging tone. 'I'll be there in a minute,' she said, and flicked off the switch.

She opened the door to the stairwell that led from the second floor to the street entrance. There were two doors at the base of the stairs, one leading to the garage that occupied the ground floor and the second to the street sidewalk.

Opening the second door, Sabrina walked four paces and stopped. There was an iron grillework gate less than a foot in front of her, preventing direct access to the house from people on the street. Bay was on the other side of that gate.

'Now, what was it you wanted, Mr. Cameron?' she asked coolly.

'May I come in?' he asked in a mocking voice.

Her common sense lost its silent war. Angry fingers unfastened the lock, swinging the gate open to allow him admittance into the small detached foyer. Sabrina stepped back, clasping her hands in front of her in a prim pose.

'Why did you want to see me?' There was a vaguely haughty arch in her long neck.

'It's what a native would consider a most unusual day. There's not a cloud in the sky. The sun is shining. The breeze is light and warm. It's the perfect day for a walk,' Bay concluded. 'I stopped to see if you'd come with me.'

Sabrina doubted the sincerity of his words. She couldn't believe that his motive for asking was a genuine desire for her company. He was feeling sorry for her.

'I'm sorry, it isn't possible,' she refused with honest cause.

'It isn't possible?' he questioned. Sabrina could visualize the arrogant lift of his brow. 'Why?'

'I'm fixing a pot roast for dinner this evening. I have to put it in the oven in —' she touched the braille face of her watch '— forty-five minutes. So you see, if I went for a walk with you, we would barely be gone and we'd have to come back. An hour after that I'll have to be here to add the potatoes, carrots and onions.'

'Is that the only excuse you have?'

'It's a very legitimate one,' Sabrina returned firmly.

'If that's your only reason, we can soon take care of that,' Bay said complacently. 'Your oven has a timer. While you're getting the roast ready, I'll set the timer to turn the oven on in forty-five minutes. We can put it in now and have nearly two hours for our walk before you have to be back to add the rest of the items.'

'But —' She tried to protest, but her mind was blank.

'But what? Don't you want to go for a walk? It's too beautiful a day to stay indoors.'

'Oh, all right,' she sighed in exasperation, turning toward the door.

His throaty chuckle mocked her obviously reluctant agreement. 'I'm amazed at how graciously you always accept my invitations,' Bay taunted.

'Maybe it's because I can't help wondering why you make them,' Sabrina responded with faint acidity in her tone.

'I have the impression,' he reached around and opened the door for her before her searching hands found the knob, 'that if you ever stopped being defensive over the fact that you're blind, you just might be pleasant company.'

Again Sabrina bridled silently at his implication that she spent too much time feeling sorry for herself. When her entire life and future had been based on the ability of her eyes to see the things her hands would paint, it was natural that she should feel bitterness at the injustice of her fate. Even Bay had acknowledged that. If he agreed, then what right did he have to condemn her?

Bay Cameron seemed to make his own laws, Sabrina decided. She ushered him silently up the stairs, through the dining room into the kitchen. By the time she had the meat seasoned and in the roasting pan, he had the oven ready.

'Are we ready to leave now?' Bay asked.

'I have to call my father.' She ran her palms nervously over the rounded curve of her hip bones.

'When Peggy Collins, our neighbor, is gone, he likes me to let him know where I'm going and when I'll be back.'

'In case some unsuspecting motorist runs you down?' he mocked.

Her mouth tightened into a mutinous line as she pivoted sharply away. 'You certainly have a thing about white canes, don't you?' she murmured sarcastically.

'I suppose so,' he agreed lazily. 'Go ahead and phone your father.'

'Thank you, I will, now that I have your permission,' Sabrina snapped.

The switchboard girl at her father's law firm put the call through to him immediately. She explained quickly that Peggy wasn't home and that she had called to let him know she was going to be out for a while, not mentioning with whom.

'How long will you be?' Grant Lane asked.

'A couple of hours. I'll call as soon as I'm back,' Sabrina assured him.

'I know the weather is nice, but do you have to be gone that long? I don't like the idea of you wandering about the streets on your own,' he said.

'I'll be all right.' She was strangely reluctant to tell him she was being accompanied by Bay Cameron. 'Don't start worrying,' she laughed nervously.

A muscled arm reached around her and took the receiver from her hand. She tried to take it back, but her hand encountered the rock wall of his chest. Her fingers drew back quickly as if burned.

'Mr. Lane, this is Bay Cameron. Sabrina will be with me. I'll see that she's back in plenty of time so that your dinner won't be ruined.' Her father made some affirmative reply, then Bay said goodbye and hung up the telephone. 'He asked me to tell you to have a good time.'

'Thanks,' she murmured caustically, and walked to the closet to get her lightweight coat.

Retrieving her cane from the umbrella stand, she heard Bay open the stair door. She walked quickly through the opening, listening to him lock the door behind him before following her down the stairs to the outer street.

'I thought we'd take the Hyde Street cable car down to Ghirardelli Square. Is that all right?' There was an underlying tone of amusement in his voice, suggesting that he found her sulking display of temper humorous.

'Whatever you like.' She shrugged her shoulders stiffly.

There was no mocking rejoinder at her less than courteous acceptance of his plan. In fact, he said not another word. If it hadn't been for the hand that took her elbow at the traffic intersections, Sabrina might have been walking the blocks to the cable car street alone. Except for a curt thank you when he helped her on to and off the cable car, she didn't address any remarks to him either.

'Are you finished pouting yet?' His question was heavy with concealed laughter as his hand firmly attached itself to her waist to maneuver them through the stream of summer tourists.

'I wasn't pouting,' Sabrina asserted coldly.

'You weren't?' Bay mocked.

'Maybe a little,' she acknowledged reluctantly, a trace of anger remaining. 'But you can be insufferably bossy at times.'

'I think you've just got your way too often lately. The people who care about you don't like to say "no," ' he observed.

'The same could be said for you.'

'I'm sure it's true.' Again there was a lazy acceptance of her criticism. 'But we weren't talking about me. You were the one who was pouting.'

'Only because you were taking over and running things without being asked,' Sabrina retorted.

'So what now? Do you maintain a state of war or take our walk as friends?' She could feel his eyes on her face. 'We didn't get along too badly the other day.'

Sabrina breathed in deeply, feeling herself surrendering to the invisible charm of his low voice. 'Friends,' she agreed against her better judgment.

Once she had succumbed it was easy to let herself be warmed by his persuasion as he gently steered the conversation to less argumentative topics. They wandered around the fountain in the center plaza of the old Ghirardelli chocolate factory renovated into a shopping mall. They stopped at one of the outdoor cafés and sampled some of the thin, delicious crepes freshly made.

Their strolling pace took them by the windows of the multi-level shops in the buildings that made up the square. Bay laughingly challenged Sabrina to identify the type of store by sound and scent. She did quite well at the flower and leather shops and identifying what native cuisine was served at the various restaurants, but the jewelry, gift and import stores she missed entirely.

When Bay stopped in front of another shop window, she emitted a defeated sigh. 'I'm really out of guesses. Please, no more.'

'No, no more,' he agreed absently. 'It's a dressmaker's shop, more specifically labelled as Original Fashions by Jacobina. There's a dress in the window, and I'd swear it was made for you. Come on.' His arm tightened suddenly around her waist. 'We'll go in so you can see it.'

Instantly Sabrina strained against his arm. 'You're overlooking one pertinent detail. I'm blind. I cannot "see" the dress,' she reminded him sharply.

33

'I've overlooked nothing, my blind queen,' he replied patiently. 'So you can wipe that look of indignation from your face. Where's all that creative imagination you were bragging about the other day? I'm taking you into the shop and you're going to see this dress with your hands.'

Feeling roundly chastised, Sabrina mutely allowed herself to be escorted into the shop. A tiny bell sounded above their heads as they walked in. Immediately footsteps approached from the rear of the store.

'May I help you?' a woman's voice inquired.

'Yes,' Bay answered. 'We'd like to look at the dress in the window.'

'We don't sell ready-made dresses here, sir,' the woman replied politely. 'It's a model from which we make another using the precise measurements of our customer.'

'Let me explain what I meant.' The velvet charm was very pronounced in his voice. 'Miss Lane is blind. I admired the dress in the window and wanted her to see it. In order for her to do that, she must touch it. Would that be possible?'

'Of course, I'm sorry. It will take me only a few minutes to remove it from the model,' the woman offered quickly and warmly.

Her words were followed by a rustle of motion and material. Sabrina shifted uncomfortably and felt the pressure of Bay's hand on her waist increase in reassurance. Short minutes later there was a silky swish of material in front of her.

'Here you are, Miss Lane,' the clerk said.

'Would you describe it for her?' Bay requested.

'Of course,' the woman agreed. 'Miss Jacobina calls this dress "Flame." Its ever-changing colors of red, gold, orange and yellow in irregular layered vees of chiffon curl at the ends like tongued flames.' Sabrina's sensitive fingers lightly traced the edges of the many layers. 'The neckline is vee-shaped but not plunging by any means. The illusion of sleeves is created by the cutaway vees of chiffon from the neckline, draping over the shoulders and the bodice.'

As the exploring tips of her fingers went over more of the dress Sabrina's mind began to form a picture with the help of the clerk's description.

'It's beautiful,' Sabrina murmured finally.

'What size is the model?' Bay asked. The woman told him. 'Would that fit you, Sabrina?'

'I think so,' she nodded.

'Can you stretch the rules to allow her to try it on?' he asked the clerk, again in that persuasive tone that Sabrina was certain no one could resist.

The woman took a deep breath, then laughed. 'I don't know why not. We have a changing room in the back. Miss Lane, if you'd like to come with me.'

Sabrina hesitated and Bay gave her a little push forward. 'Go on. Let's see what it looks like on,' he prompted.

'Why do I let you talk me into these situations?' she sighed.

'Because deep down, you enjoy it,' he teased. 'Besides, I bet you haven't bought any new clothes since the accident.'

'I haven't needed anything,' Sabrina protested weakly.

'When has that ever been a valid excuse for a woman?' Bay mocked. 'Now, go try that dress on. That's an order!'

'Yes, sir.' She didn't really have to have her arm twisted. The vision in her mind and the touch of the expensive material already had her excited about wearing it, even if she couldn't see the end result.

Changing swiftly out of her sports clothes into the dress, she only required the assistance of the clerk with the zipper. With her hand resting lightly on the clerk's arm, she moved nervously to the front of the store where Bay waited.

'Well?' Sabrina asked breathlessly when the silence stretched to an unbearable length. Her head was tilted to one side in a listening attitude.

'You look beautiful, Sabrina,' Bay said simply.

'That's an understatement,' the clerk inserted. 'You're stunning, and I'm not saying that because I work here. The dress might have been made for you. The style, the color suits you perfectly. It's amazing, but you must have the same measurements as the girl who models it.'

Her fingers ran down the neckline of the dress, trailing off with a draping fold of the filmy chiffon. 'Could you — would you sell this one?' Sabrina asked.

'It's not customary,' the woman hesitated, then added with a resigned smile in her voice. 'Let me check.'

When the woman had left, Sabrina turned again to Bay. 'Are you very sure it looks right?' she questioned anxiously.

There was a click, then cigarette smoke wafted through the air to her nose. 'Are you seeking more compliments?' he asked.

'No,' she denied, nervously running her hand along the waist and glancing sightlessly at the floating vees of material cascading over her arm. 'It's just that I can't be positive —'

'Be positive.' With cat-soft footsteps he was at her side, lifting her chin with his finger. 'I told you the truth. You look beautiful in the dress.'

She wished she could see his expression. The sincerity in his voice she didn't doubt, but there was an illusive sensation that he was aloof, withdrawn. The fringe of dark hair hid the tiny frown that knitted her forehead.

'Now what's troubling you?' Bay mocked.

'I —' Her chin was released as he stepped away. 'I was just wondering when I would ever wear this,' Sabrina hedged at the truth.

'Sometime there'll be an occasion when the dress will be just right for it. Then you'll be glad you bought it,' he replied in an indulgent tone.

'I never asked how much it is,' she murmured. Then an accompanying thought dropped her shoulders. 'I have hardly any money with me. Do you suppose I could give them some money to hold it and Daddy and I could come down later with the rest?'

'I could pay for it,' Bay suggested guardedly.

Sabrina bit into her lower lip, eager to possess the dress she wore but unwilling to obligate herself to a man who was neither friend nor stranger.

'If it wouldn't be too much trouble,' her acceptance was hesitant, 'you could write down your address and the amount. I'll have Dad mail you a check tonight.'

'You wouldn't consider accepting the dress as a gift?'

Sabrina drew back. 'No.' She shook her head firmly, ready to argue the point further if he should attempt to bully her into accepting it.

'I didn't think you would.' A rush of smoke was exhaled in her direction. He sounded vaguely angry. 'All right, I'll *loan* you the money for the dress.'

'Thank you,' breathed Sabrina, relieved the episode was not going to end on a quarrelsome note.

'Instead of your father mailing me a check, why don't I stop by your house Friday afternoon?' he suggested.

'If you like,' she frowned.

'I would like.' The smile was back in his voice and she gave him an answering one.

The sales clerk returned with the information that they would sell the dress model to Sabrina. The price of the garment was not as high as she had expected. While she changed into her denim slacks and top, Bay took care of the purchase.

Outside the store he gave her the unwelcome news that they had used up the two hours and it was time for him to take her back to the house. He suggested that instead of taking the cable car, then walking the several blocks to her house, that they take a taxi. At this point, Sabrina would have preferred to prolong the outing, but there had been a subtle change in his attitude, so she agreed to his suggestion.

'I'll see you Friday afternoon around two,' Bay repeated, stopping inside the iron gate but not following her into the stairwell.

'Would y-you like to come in for coffee?' she offered.

'I'll take a raincheck on that for Friday,' he refused.

'All right. Till Friday, then,' Sabrina agreed with a faint smile of regret.

Four

Sabrina touched the face of her watch. Two o'clock. She reached to be certain the check was still on the coffee table where her father had put it this morning. It was. She leaned against the cushion of the couch, rubbing the back of her neck to try to relax the tense muscles. It was crazy to be so on edge because Bay Cameron was coming over, she told herself.

The front buzzer sounded and she hurried to the intercom, answering it with an eager 'Yes?'

'Bay Cameron.'

'I'll be right down.'

Recklessly Sabrina nearly flew down the stairs. A smile wreathed her face as she opened the door and walked to the gate.

'You're right on time,' she said.

'I try to be punctual.' The warm huskiness of his voice swept over her as she unlocked the gate, swinging the iron grille open to admit him.

'I have the coffee all ready if you have time to stay,' she offered.

'I have time,' Bay answered.

Leading the way up the stairs to the second floor living area, Sabrina motioned toward the living room. 'Have a seat while I get the coffee tray. The check for the dress is on the table in front of the sofa.'

Bay made no offer to help pour the coffee when she returned, letting her take the time to do it herself. He took the cup she held out to him, the almost silent swish of the cushions indicating that he had leaned back against the chair next to the sofa.

'You have a very nice home. The paintings on the wall, are they yours?' he asked.

'Yes,' she acknowledged, carefully balancing a cup in her lap. 'My father likes landscapes, so he chose those for the house. Because of his love for the sea, they are actually ocean scenes.'

'Are these the only paintings of your own that you have left?'

Sabrina bent her head. 'No.' Her jaw tightened.

'May I see them later?' Bay requested with watching softness.

'I'd really rather not show them to you.' She swallowed, lifting her chin defiantly.

'If you'd rather not, I won't insist,' he shrugged. 'But I won't pretend that I'm not curious why. I've already seen several examples of your work. Why wouldn't you want to show me the rest?'

Sabrina fidgeted nervously with the handle of her cup. Trying to adopt an uncaring attitude, she set the cup on the table.

'I'll show them to you.' Not certain whether her change of mind had been prompted by the patiently humorous tone of his voice or an application of common sense. 'They're in the studio upstairs.' She rose to her feet, pausing to turn her head in the direction of his chair.

'Lead the way,' Bay agreed, now on his feet, too.

Climbing the stairs to the upper floor, Sabrina trailed her hand along the wall until she came to the second door. The knob was cold beneath her fingers as she swung the door open. The lingering scent of oil paints whirled around her.

'The room isn't used — any more, so it might be a bit stuffy,' Sabrina explained self-consciously, halting against the wall just inside the door.

Bay didn't comment. It wasn't really necessary. She listened to the quiet sounds as he wandered about the room, pausing sometimes to take a closer look at something that had caught his eye. Other times she could hear him moving canvases to see the paintings behind them. A tightness gripped her chest with a painful hold.

'They're very good, Sabrina,' he said at last. Her head turned in the direction of his voice only a few feet from where she was standing near the door. 'It's a pity to keep them hidden in this room.'

'Dad and I have talked about selling them. We will some day.' Sabrina swallowed to ease the constriction in her throat.

'Did you ever do any modeling?'

'Modeling? No,' she replied, striving for a lightness even though she knew neither of them would be fooled by it. 'I was always the one painting the person who was posing.'

'I meant modeling in clay,' Bay explained. Quiet, unhurried footsteps brought him to her side. A hand lightly touched her arm to turn her toward the open door.

'Yes, when I was studying the different mediums of art,' Sabrina acknowledged with a slight frown. 'Why?'

'Have you ever considered taking it up now that you're blind?'

'No.' She shook her head.

Unconsciously she had allowed him to lead her into the hallway. His inquiry had been unexpected and it set off a chain of thoughts. The closing of the studio door brought her back to their surroundings.

The subject was not explored further as Bay let her descend the stairs ahead of him, deliberately allowing her to mull the idea over in her own mind without any attempt to influence her. In spite of an ego-born desire to reject the idea to do anything but her chosen field of painting, the seed had been planted in fertile ground.

The coffee Sabrina poured had grown cold. While she emptied the cups, there was more time to contemplate his indirect suggestion. She marveled that none of her art friends had mentioned it before. Perhaps the objectivity of a relative stranger had been needed.

'I meant to ask,' Bay said as Sabrina handed him his cup refilled with hot coffee, 'whether you and your father had any plans for tomorrow evening.'

Her own cup was half-filled, the coffee pot poised above it for a startled split second. 'No,' Sabrina answered in a curious tone. 'Saturday afternoon and evening Dad spends with Deborah. Why?'

'I thought we could have dinner somewhere. It would give you an excuse to wear your new dress,' Bay answered smoothly.

'No, thank you,' she refused with cutting abruptness.

'Do you have other plans?'

'No.'

'Then may I ask why you don't want to have dinner with me?' he asked, completely unruffled by her cold rejection.

'You may.' With a proud set to her head, Sabrina replaced the coffeepot on the tray and leaned against the sofa, protectively cradling the cup in her hands. 'I simply don't eat at public restaurants. I have a habit of knocking over glasses and dropping food on the floor. It's embarrassing,' she concluded self-consciously.

'I'm willing to take the risk,' Bay returned.

'Well, I'm not.' Impatiently she took a sip of the hot liquid, nearly scalding her tongue in the process.

'If this is not a refusal of my company,' there was a hint of amusement in his voice, 'then would you consider a less formal suggestion? For instance, we could buy some shrimp and crab at the Wharf, sourdough bread and a salad of sorts, then have an impromptu picnic somewhere along the shore line of the Golden Gate Promenade.'

Sabrina hesitated. It sounded like fun, but she wasn't certain she should accept his invitation. In between the moments when she was angered by his arrogance, she had discovered she liked him. Yet she doubted if any enduring friendship would ever develop between them.

'Is it such a difficult invitation to accept?' Bay taunted.

His gentle mockery made her feel foolish. She was magnifying the importance of the invitation out of all proportion. A faint pink tinted her prominent cheekbones.

'It isn't difficult,' she murmured, bending her head toward the cup in her lap to hide the flush of embarrassment. 'I do accept.'

'Would six o'clock be all right, or would you rather have me come earlier?'

'Six is fine.' There was a thump from something falling to the floor. Her head jerked up with a start. 'What was that?'

'It's a little something I bought for you as a present,' Bay replied with studied casualness. 'I meant to give it to you earlier, but I got sidetracked. I had it propped against my chair and I accidentally knocked it over. Here you are.'

A long, narrow box was placed on her lap after Sabrina had set her coffee cup on the table. Her hands rested motionless on the cardboard lid.

'Why did you buy me a present?' she asked warily.

'Because I wanted to — and please don't ask me to take it back, because I wouldn't have any use for it and neither would anyone else I know. I doubt if I can have it returned either,' he stated.

'What is it?' Sabrina tilted her head curiously to the side.

'You'll have to open it and find out for yourself,' Bay answered noncommittally.

With a trace of nervous excitement hampering her movements, Sabrina eased the lid off the box and set it on the sofa. She could feel his alert gaze watching her. Her pulse accelerated slightly. Hesitantly exploring fingertips encountered tissue paper. It rustled softly as she pushed it aside to find what it protected.

The object in the box was round and hard. Initially the cylindrical object was unidentifiable until Sabrina felt along its length. Her hand had barely curled around it to lift it out of the box and she replaced it, folding her hands tightly in her lap. A sickening sensation curled her stomach.

'It's a white cane, isn't it?' she accused tightly, a bad taste bitterly coating her tongue as she uttered the words.

'Yes,' Bay admitted without any trace of remorse. 'But I like to think it isn't an ordinary white cane.'

The box was removed from her lap. The action was followed almost instantly by the rustling of tissue paper, then the sound of the box being set aside. Her lips were compressed tightly shut in an uncompromising line while her hands maintained their death grip on each other. Bay's fingers closed over her wrist and firmly pulled her hands apart, ignoring the resistance she offered.

One hand he released. The second he held with little effort. The curving handle of the cane was pressed into her palm and Bay forced her fingers to curl around it.

Sabrina's first impression was of a smooth glassy surface, then her sensitive touch felt the carving. Almost unwillingly her fingertips explored the design. It was several seconds before she followed the intricate serpentine lines flanking the sides of the cane to the end of the handle. There she was able to identify the design of reptilian heads as those of a dragon.

'It's a cane carved out of ivory,' Bay explained. 'I saw it in a shop window in Chinatown the other day.'

'It's very beautiful,' Sabrina admitted reluctantly. The hand covering hers relaxed its grip, no longer forcing her to hold on to the cane. She held on to it for a few more exploring moments. 'It must be valuable,' she commented, and extended it toward him. 'I couldn't possibly accept it.'

'It's artistic in design but hardly an art object.' He ignored the outstretched hand with the cane. 'What you really mean is it's still white.'

Sabrina didn't deny his charge. 'I can't accept it.'

'I can't return it,' Bay replied evenly.

'I'm sorry.' She pushed the cane into his hands and released it. He had no choice but to hold on to it or let it fall to the floor.

'I know you were trying to be thoughtful, but you knew my views on the subject of canes before you bought it, Bay. The cane is unique and beautiful, but I won't accept it. I get along very well with the one I have.'

'Is that your final answer?'

'Yes, it is,' Sabrina answered firmly, resolved not to be bullied or made to feel guilty because she had refused.

'I suppose if I try to persuade you to change your mind, you'll go back on your agreement to go out with me tomorrow night,' he sighed with almost resigned acceptance.

'Probably,' she shrugged, hoping he wouldn't put her in such a position.

'Then I'll save my arguments for another time.' There was a rustle of tissue paper and the lid being placed on the box. 'Mind you, I'm not giving up,' Bay warned mockingly, 'just postponing the battle.'

'I won't change my mind,' Sabrina replied stubbornly but with a trace of a smile curling her wide mouth.

'I accept the challenge.' She could hear the answering smile in his voice. 'While we're still on speaking terms, may I have another cup of coffee?'

'Of course.' She held out her hand for his cup and saucer.

The subject of the ivory cane was not re-introduced into the conversation, but when Bay Cameron left a half an hour later, Sabrina made certain he had the box with him and did not 'accidentally' forget it.

It was not until that evening when Deborah came that Sabrina discovered the way Bay had tricked her.

'When did you get this, Sabrina?' Deborah asked in a voice that was at one and the same time curious and surprised.

Her fingers stopped their braille reading in mid-sentence as she turned her head in the direction of Deborah's voice. 'What is it?'

'An ivory cane. The handle has a dragon design carved on the sides. I found it on the floor beside the chair. Were you hiding it?' The red-haired woman laughed shortly.

'No, I wasn't.' Sabrina's mouth thinned grimly.

'It's very elegant. Where did you find it?' Deborah murmured.

'Yes, where?' her father joined in. 'I haven't seen it before. Is this something else you found the other day when you were with Bay Cameron?'

'You should know by now, Father, that I would never buy a white cane, much less an ivory one,' she retorted. 'It was a present from Bay. I refused it, of course. I thought he had taken it with him.'

'Refused it?' Deborah questioned in amazement. 'Why would you refuse something as lovely as this?'

'Because I don't want it,' Sabrina answered tautly.

The sofa cushion beside her sank as it took her father's weight. His hand gently covered the rigid fingers resting on the now closed cover of her book.

'Aren't you being a little foolish, honey?' The chiding question was spoken softly. 'We both know you didn't refuse it because you thought it was too expensive or because you didn't think it was beautiful. It's because it's white. And a white cane means that you're blind. You can't escape the fact that you're blind simply by not using a white cane.'

'I don't wish to advertise the fact,' was her curt reply.

'People are bound to notice, no matter what kind or color of cane you have. There's no shame in being blind, for heaven's sake,' Grant Lane argued.

'I'm not ashamed!' Sabrina snapped.

'Sometimes you act as if you are,' he sighed.

'I suppose you think I should use it,' she challenged with a defiant toss of her head.

'I'm your father, Sabrina. Take the chip off your shoulder.' The mildly reproving tone of his voice lessened the jutting angle of her chin. 'You're too old for me to tell you what to do. You know what the right and wise thing to do is. Whether you do it or not is your decision.'

'Excuse me, I think I'll go to my room.' Sabrina set the book on the table and rose stiffly to her feet.

It was impossible to argue when her father wouldn't argue back. She hated it when he appealed to her logic. She invariably lost.

'What should I do with the cane?' Deborah inquired hesitantly.

'Put it in the umbrella stand for now,' her father answered. 'Sabrina can decide what she wants to do before Bay Cameron comes over tomorrow night.'

As Sabrina put her foot on the first step of the stairs leading to the upper floor and her bedroom, she heard Deborah ask, 'Bay Cameron is coming tomorrow night. Why?'

'He's taking Sabrina to the Wharf,' her father replied.

'You mean a date?' his fiancée asked with amazed disbelief.

'I suppose you could call it that. He called me yesterday afternoon at the office after he'd seen Sabrina to ask if I had any objection. I couldn't bring myself to ask him what his intentions were. It would have been too presumptuous when he's been kind to her.'

'Did he mention the cane?'

'No, it was a complete surprise to me,' he answered.

Well, Sabrina sighed in relief, at least her father hadn't been a part of any conspiracy with Bay Cameron. For a moment, she had been worried. She should have realized her father wouldn't do anything underhanded to trick her into making the decision he wanted. It was a pity the same couldn't be said for Bay Cameron.

Still, she had to concede that Bay had not forced her to accept the ivory cane. He had simply left it. And its presence had produced another dilemma, thanks to her father.

A few minutes before six o'clock, Sabrina sat on the sofa, nibbling on the tip of one fingernail. She absently reached out for the second time to be certain the hooded blue windbreaker was lying on the arm of the sofa. Then her pensive mood was broken by the front door buzzer.

Quickly she pulled on the windbreaker, stuffing the small clutch purse in its oversize pocket. A smoothing hand ran up the back of her neck, tucking any stray strands of hair into the knot atop her head. Her inquiry via the intercom was answered, as she had expected, by Bay.

'I'll be right down,' she murmured.

Her hand closed over the doorknob, but she hesitated. Her sightless eyes stared at the umbrella stand. Her other hand was poised on the smooth oak cane. For several more seconds she remained immobile, then with a resigned sigh, she removed her hand from the oak cane and tentatively searched for the carved dragon heads of the ivory cane.

Slowly she descended the stairs, opening the outside door and locking it behind her. Squaring her shoulders, she turned toward the iron gates and Bay.

'You took your time,' he commented. 'I was beginning to wonder what was keeping you.'

'I had to put on my jacket,' Sabrina lied, waiting for him to comment on the ivory cane in her hand.

'My car is parked at the curb,' Bay said as she swung open the gates and joined him on the sidewalk.

The hand on her elbow firmly guided her to the car. The suspense of waiting for his expression of triumph began to build as he helped her into the car. When Bay had still said nothing after the car was started and turned into the street, Sabrina knew she could not continue waiting for a moment of his choosing.

'Well?' she challenged finally, turning her head toward him in a slightly defiant angle.

'Well what?' Bay countered evenly.

'Aren't you going to say anything about the cane?'

'What do you expect me to say?' The low, calm voice remained controlled and unruffled.

'I should think you'd be feeling pretty smug. After all, you did leave the cane behind deliberately,' Sabrina accused.

'I gave it to you. It was a present, and I don't take back presents. It was entirely up to you what you did with it. I never insisted that you use it. I wouldn't have stopped you if you'd thrown it in the garbage,' responded Bay.

'Well, I have decided to use it,' she stated, facing straight ahead.

'I'm glad.' The car turned and went steeply down a hill. 'May we leave the subject of the cane behind now?'

Sabrina sighed, 'Yes.'

It seemed as if every time she thought she knew how he would react, Bay did not do the expected. He should have been triumphant or a little righteous. Instead he was so calm and matter-of-fact that it was impossible for Sabrina to feel resentment. She had made the decision to use the ivory cane, not Bay, and he knew it.

At the bottom of the inclining street, Bay turned the car again. 'I thought I'd park at the Yacht Harbor. We can follow the sea-wall by Fort Mason to Aquatic Park and on to Fisherman's Wharf. All right?'

'Fine,' Sabrina agreed.

Once the car was parked and locked, they started out at a strolling pace with Bay hooking Sabrina's left arm under his right. Gulls screeched overhead. As they passed Fort Mason and neared the docks of the fishing fleet, the heavier flapping wings of pelicans accompanied the soaring seagulls. The damp salt odor of the air was altered by a fishy smell.

Although the seafood stalls were their ultimate destination, they mutually decided to walk farther and come back. The sidewalks were filled with tourists exploring the sights and sounds of the colorful area. A few were jostling and in a hurry but most took their time absorbing the atmosphere as Sabrina and Bay were doing.

The churning propellers of a tour boat indicated the start of another harbor cruise. The highlights would be a close look at the famed Golden Gate Bridge, the Oakland Bay Bridge and the former maximum security prison of Alcatraz. Now the island was a national park, only a mile out in the bay from the wharf.

At the end of the piers, they crossed the street to the rows of shops and started slowly back toward the seafood stalls.

Sabrina lifted her face to the breeze, salty and damp. 'Is the fog coming in?'

'Starting,' Bay agreed. 'It's just beginning to obscure the top spans of the Golden Gate and the Marin hills north of the Bay. It might get thick tonight.'

'In that case, I'll have to lead you back to the car,' she grinned impishly, and Bay chuckled. Sabrina tipped her head curiously toward him. 'Where did you get the name Bay?'

'My parents gave it to me — or didn't you think I had any?' he teased.

'Of course I did. Are they still living?' she asked, sidetracked momentarily from her original question.

'Last I heard they were. They're in Europe taking a second honeymoon.' His arm tightened fractionally in warning. 'You have to step down here.'

'Is Bay a family name?' Sabrina questioned again after negotiating the intersection curb.

'I wish it were. No, I was named after the obvious, the San Francisco Bay that my mother saw from the hospital window. She was born and raised here, so she'd seen it thousands of times,' he explained. 'What about Sabrina?'

'My mother liked the sound of it. She was very romantic.'

'And you're not?' he mocked.

'Maybe a little bit,' she smiled faintly.

'We've been walking for over an hour. Are you getting hungry?' Bay inquired with an easy change of the subject.

'Very close to starving.'

'You should have said something sooner.'

Sabrina shrugged that it didn't matter and breathed in the tantalizing aroma carried by the light breeze. 'It's just across the street, isn't it?' Then she laughed. 'All I have to do is follow my nose.'

'Are you certain you wouldn't rather eat in one of the restaurants here?' Bay checked her movement into the street and a car drove slowly by.

'Positive,' bobbing her head firmly.

At the long row of seafood stalls, Bay selected the cooked crab, including a round loaf of sourdough bread, a salad and cocktail shrimp to the order. Sabrina pressed a hand against her rumbling stomach. The delicious smells were making her all the more hungry. With the purchase completed, Bay handed her the bag and asked her to wait outside while he bought a bottle of chilled white wine to go with it.

Tingles ran down the back of her neck an instant before his hand touched her arm signaling his return. She decided that she must have telepathic powers that told her when Bay approached.

'Are you ready for our picnic?' he asked. At that moment her stomach growled the answer and they both laughed.

Taking the bag of food from her grasp, Bay added it to the one he already had in his arms. The hand she linked in his arm was not for guidance but companionship as they set out for the Yacht Harbor and the shoreline beyond.

They were on the edge of the harbor when Sabrina noticed the fine mist on her face had intensified. 'It's drizzling rain,' she moaned angrily.

'I was afraid it was an overcast more than fog,' Bay sighed.

'I suppose we could always take the food to the house,' Sabrina suggested.

'I have a better idea. My ketch is tied up here. We can eat aboard her. What do you say?'

'I say,' she smiled, 'that it sounds much more pleasant than my house.'

'Let's go!'

Bay had Sabrina wait on the dock while he stowed the food below. Topside again, his strong hands spanned her waist and lifted her aboard. He maintained the hold for steadying minutes, her own hands resting on the rippling muscles of his forearms. The dampness of the drizzling rain increased the spicy aroma emanating from his shaven cheeks and the heady male that enfolded her. The deck beneath her feet moved rhythmically with the lapping waters of the bay.

'It's been so long since I've been on the water,' Sabrina said with an odd catch in her voice, 'that my sea-legs are a bit shaky.' It seemed a reasonable explanation for the weakness in her limbs.

With an arm firmly circling her waist in support, Bay led her below deck. Making certain she had something to hold on to, he went down the steps ahead of her. Sabrina knew it was to catch her in case she fell. Once below he told her where the seats were and let her make her own way to them.

'Do you like sailing?' he asked. The rustling of bags indicated he was getting the food out to eat.

'Love it.' A wry grimace pulled down the corners of her mouth in a rueful expression. 'I used to go out every weekend with Dad.'

'You haven't been out since your accident? Why?' His low voice was honed sharp with curiosity.

'Oh, a couple of times, but I had to stay below. Dad can't swim. He was afraid I would fall overboard and he wouldn't be able to save me. I like to be on deck where the salt wind stings your face and the waves breaking over the bow spray you. So I don't go out any more,' she concluded.

'And you aren't afraid of falling in?'

'Not really,' Sabrina shrugged.

A shrimp cocktail was set before her as Bay took a seat opposite her. For a time the conversation centered around sailing, then shifted smoothly to other topics of interest, mainly leisure activities, as they slowly ate their picnic meal.

'I used to really enjoy watching people, studying their faces.' She sipped lightly at the wine. 'Of course, I did it often in connection with my work. Most of my better characters came from the faces of people I saw on the streets. A great deal of a person's attitude toward life is written on his face. The grumpy look of a pessimist, the hardness

49

of a cynic, the authority of a leader, the harried worn look of a man driven to succeed, an eagerness for life, the contentment of family and home. There are so many things,' Sabrina exhaled slowly. 'It's not so easy to do it with just voices, but I'm learning. It's difficult, though, to visualize a person's looks from their voice.'

'What have you learned about me?' Bay challenged mockingly.

'Well,' a hint of mischief tickled the corners of her mouth, 'you're self-confident to the point of arrogance. You're well-educated, accustomed to having authority over others. You obviously enjoy the outdoors and especially the sea. You have a quick temper, but you can be thoughtful when it suits you.'

'Have you put a face with my voice yet?'

Sabrina quickly ducked her head from his gaze self-consciously. 'Only a blurred image of strong features.' She pushed her plate away. 'That was good.'

'Why haven't you asked to look at me?' Bay asked quietly, ignoring her attempt to switch the subject to food.

'W-what?' she stammered.

'As you did with the dress,' he explained patiently.

Humor hovered on the edge of his voice after she had shifted uncomfortably in her seat. The thought of exploring his face with her hands was disturbing.

'I could fill in the blank spots for you. I have green hair and purple eyes, a long ugly scar down the side of my face. I keep it hidden with a bushy green beard. I have a tattoo of a skull and crossbones on my forehead — and I won't tell you what the picture is on my chest.' The spreading smile on Sabrina's face broke into laughter at his absurd description. 'Don't you believe me?'

'Hardly. Besides, my neighbor's already told me you have reddish-brown hair and eyes,' Sabrina laughed, her tension fading.

'Cinnamon, according to my mother,' Bay corrected. 'At least you were curious enough about me to ask.'

'Naturally.' She worked to make her reply sound casual and offhand.

'What else did she tell you about me?' he prodded.

'Peggy isn't very good at describing,' Sabrina hedged, unwilling to pass on the comment concerning his masculinity.

'All the more reason for you to see for yourself,' he challenged.

There was the clatter of plates being stacked, then movement as the dishes were carried away. Bay's actions gave her time to think of an excuse to avoid the exploration of his features that he had invited. Try as she could, Sabrina was unable to come up with one that did not reveal her inner apprehension at such intimacy.

When Bay returned, he did not take his former seat across from her but one that placed him beside her. Before she could voice her half-formed protest, he had taken her wrists in a light yet firm grip and carried her hands to his face.

'There's no need to feel shy and self-conscious,' he scolded gently as she tried to pull away. 'It doesn't embarrass me.'

The hard outline of his powerful jaw was beneath her hands, pressed by his on either side of his face. As her resistance faded, he released his hold. The initial contact had been made and the warmth of his body heat eased the cold stiffness of her fingers. Tentatively Sabrina began to explore his face.

From the jawline, her fingertips searched over his cheeks to the hard angles of his cheekbones. Fluttering over the curling lashes of his eyes, she reached thick brows and the wide forehead. Thick, slightly waving hair grew naturally away from his face, maintaining a suggestion of dampness from the fog and the drizzle. There was an arrogant curve to his Roman nose and a gentle firmness to his male lips. After inspecting the almost forceful angle of his chin, her hands fell away.

It was a masculine face, Sabrina thought in satisfaction. There was no doubt about that. No one would ever refer to him as conventionally handsome, but he was certainly striking. Heads would turn when he walked into a room.

'What's the verdict?' Bay asked in a husky caressing voice like deep velvet.

She guessed her approval was mirrored in her expression. She averted her head slightly from the warm gaze she felt on her face.

'The verdict is,' she answered with false lightness, 'that I like your face.'

A finger tucked itself under her chin and turned her head back toward him. 'I like your face, too,' he murmured softly.

The warm moistness of his breath caressed her cheek a warning instant before his lips touched hers. Initial surprise held Sabrina rigid under his kiss, but the gently firm pressure of his mouth transmitted a warmness that seeped into her veins. Her heart seemed to start skipping beats. With expert persuasion, his mouth moved mobilely against hers until he evoked the pliant response he wanted. Then slowly, almost regretfully, he drew away from her.

Sabrina could still feel the imprint of his mouth throbbing on hers. She had to resist the impulse to carry a hand to her lips. A wondrously satisfying warmth filled her, leaving her bemused to its cause.

'Why the pensive look, Sabrina?' Bay's husky voice inquired gently.

'I've . . . never been kissed before,' she murmured, uncertain if that was the cause.

'Liar,' he mocked softly. 'That was no inexperienced maiden who kissed me back just now.'

'I — I meant,' crimson flames stained her cheeks, 'since I lost my sight.'

'That I will believe.' Bay took hold of her hand in a casual, not intimate grip. 'Let's go get ourselves a cup of coffee at a restaurant somewhere.'

Sabrina willingly agreed to leave his ketch. For some reason the floor beneath her feet didn't feel very steady. She wanted the security of solid ground beneath her.

It was a few minutes past ten o'clock when Bay parked the car in front of her house and walked her to the grillework gates. He didn't follow her inside the small enclosure and Sabrina turned to him hesitantly.

'I've had a wonderful time. Thank you,' she offered.

'So did I, therefore no thanks are necessary,' Bay said with a smile in his voice. 'I'll be in L.A. all of next week. I'll give you a call when I get back.'

'It isn't necessary.' Sabrina didn't want him to think that he was under any obligation to see her again.

'I know that,' he chided gently. 'Goodnight, Sabrina. I'll wait in the car until I see the light on upstairs, so be sure to turn it on, will you?'

'Goodnight, Bay,' she nodded.

He swung the iron gate closed and Sabrina locked it. She felt his gaze follow her to the door. Cinnamon brown eyes they were, to go with his cinnamon hair.

Five

The switch on the stereo was snapped abruptly to the 'off' position. There was nothing soothing to the music as far as Sabrina was concerned.

What was there to do, she wondered tiredly. She did not feel like cooking or cleaning even if it was needed, which it wasn't. She was tired of reading. Besides, her fingers were still slow to read the raised braille letters, so the task required her total concentration. In this restless mood, she knew her thoughts would wander.

An inner voice unfairly blamed the mood on Bay Cameron. Although why his business trip to Los Angeles should affect her this way, Sabrina didn't know. These restless moods had been with her before anyway, even before her accident. Then she had channeled the surging energy into her paintings. Now there was no outlet.

'Have you ever done any modeling — in clay, I mean?'

Bay's voice spoke clearly in her mind as if he was standing beside her. The seed that had been planted several days ago began to germinate.

Walking to the telephone, Sabrina felt for the receiver, picked it up, then hesitated. Before she changed her mind, she dialed the number. Excitement pulsated through her veins at the sound of the first ring.

'Art Supplies,' a voice answered on the second ring.

'Sam Carlysle, please,' Sabrina requested. Her fingers nervously twined around the corkscrew curl of the telephone cord. A few minutes later a familiar male voice came on the line. 'Hello, Sam. This is Sabrina.'

'Sabrina, how are you?' he exclaimed in glad surprise. Then his tone changed immediately to contriteness. 'Listen, I'm sorry I haven't phoned or stopped by for so long, but what with one thing or another —'

'That's all right,' she interrupted quickly. 'Actually I was calling to see if you could do me a favor.'

'Name it and it's yours, Sabrina.'

'I wondered if you could send someone over today with some artist's modeling clay and an inexpensive set of tools?'

'Are you taking up modeling?' he asked in a stunned voice.

'I'm going to give it a try,' Sabrina acknowledged. 'That's why I only want the bare necessities to see if I'm going to like it or be any good at it.'

'I think it's a tremendous idea!' Sam enthused. 'A stroke of genius!'

'Can you send someone over?'

'I'd come myself if I could, but I'll have a delivery boy leave here in about ten minutes and I'll make sure your place is his first stop.'

'Thanks, Sam.' A contented glow spread over her face.

'Hey, listen, I'm just sorry I didn't suggest something like this to you before,' he replied, shrugging aside her thanks. 'I'll get this stuff out to you right away. We'll get together soon, okay?'

'Yes, Sam, soon,' Sabrina agreed.

Barely a half an hour had elapsed when the delivery was made. She had already cleared a small area in the studio where she could work, realizing that her father would have to give her a hand this evening with the heavier items. The delivery man had thoughtfully offered to carry the packages wherever Sabrina wanted them so she hadn't had to carry them to the studio.

After he had left and she had returned to the studio, a thrill of excitement danced down her spine. Her old smock was behind the door, smelling of oil paints and cleaning fluid. Soon, the odor of clay would wipe out that smell, she told herself gaily as she donned the protective smock and felt her way to the work table.

All conception of time vanished. She started out with simple shapes, using fruit she had taken from the kitchen for her hands to use as a guideline. Her name was called for the third time before it penetrated her concentration. It was another full second before she recognized her father's voice.

'I'm upstairs in the studio!' she answered.

She stepped back, wiping her hands on a rag as she listened to his hurrying steps up the stairs. A look of apprehension and excitement was in the expression Sabrina turned to the open doorway.

'I was getting frantic,' Grant Lane declared with an exasperated sigh. 'Why didn't you answer me? What are you doing up here anyway?'

'Working,' Sabrina replied softly, but she could tell by the tense silence that her explanation wasn't necessary. Her father had already looked beyond her and seen for himself. She waited interminable seconds for his comment. 'What do you think?' she asked breathlessly.

'I . . . I'm speechless,' he told her. 'How — when . . . ?' Then he laughed at his inability to get his questions out and came the rest of the way into the room, throwing an arm about her shoulders and giving her a fierce hug. 'You are one fantastic little gal. I'm proud of you.' His voice was choked with emotion.

'Yes, but what do you think?' she repeated anxiously.

'If you're asking whether I can tell the apple from the pear, the answer is a definite "yes." I can even see that's a cluster of grapes you're working on now,' her father smiled. 'And I didn't need that assortment of real fruit spotted with clay to make the identification either!'

'Do you mean it?'

'I mean it,' he assured her firmly. 'Now how about an explanation? When did you decide to do all this? You never mentioned a word about it to me. Where did you get all this?'

'Last week Bay asked if I'd ever worked in clay. I guess that's when I started thinking about it, subconsciously at least. This morning I decided to try it and called Sam at the art supply store. He had this delivered for me,' Sabrina explained.

'This morning? And you've been working ever since? You must be exhausted!'

'Exhausted?' She turned her face to him, her wide mouth smiling broadly. 'No, Daddy, I'm alive. For the first time in a very long while.'

There was a moment of silence. Then her father took a deep breath. 'Just the same, you'd better call it a day. No sense in overdoing it. You clean up here and I'll see about the dinner you forgot,' he teased.

'All right,' she submitted.

For the rest of the week, Sabrina spent every waking minute she possibly could in the studio room. The end results were more often failures than successes. It didn't do any good for her father to insist that she couldn't expect to be perfect as a beginner. But Sabrina demanded perfection of herself. Nothing less would satisfy her.

On Sunday morning, Grant Lane ordered her out of the studio. 'For heaven's sake, Sabrina,' he declared, 'even God rested on the seventh day!'

The mutinous set of her chin dipped as she sighed her reluctant surrender to his logic. Her fingers ached to feel the molding clay beneath her hands, but she knew her father was right.

'I've got some work to do on the boat. Why don't you come with me this morning?' he suggested. 'Deborah is going to be busy in the kitchen. If you have nothing to do, I know you're going to sneak back up here the minute I leave.'

'I wouldn't do that,' Sabrina laughed softly.

'Oh, wouldn't you?' he mocked. 'You're coming with me.'

'I think it's awful that you don't trust me, your own daughter!' She clicked her tongue in reproval. 'But if that's the way you're going to be, I guess I'll have to go with you.'

'There's a pretty stiff breeze blowing in from the Pacific, so dress accordingly. But make sure it's something you won't mind getting dirty,' her father added. 'I thought I'd put you to work cleaning below deck.'

'That's why you want me to come along,' Sabrina nodded sagely.

'You don't think it was your company I was wanting, did you?' he teased, and walked to the stairs.

The wind was chilly, Sabrina discovered. It had not yet blown away the morning fog, so the sun had not warmed the air. Below deck, she didn't feel the cool breeze. Wiping the perspiration from her forehead that had separated her dark silky bangs into damp strands, she wished she could feel it.

She pushed up the sleeves on her navy blue pullover and set to work scrubbing the galley sink. The perspiration was making the wool blend of the turtleneck collar tickle the sensitive skin of her neck, but she couldn't very well scratch it with her soapy hands. As soon as she finished this, Sabrina decided she would call her father down for a cup of coffee. From the sound of voices overhead, he was doing more chatting with fellow sailing enthusiasts than work.

Maybe she should take the pot of coffee and some cups on deck and offer it around. There was a waterproof tin of cookies in the cupboard. Then she smiled to herself. That would really make certain nothing was accomplished today!

The quiet step of rubber-soled shoes approached the steps leading below. Sabrina was rinsing the soap from the sink when they began their descent. She stopped, turning slightly in the direction of the footsteps.

'I thought I would bring some coffee up as soon as I finish here, Dad. I'll bring some extra cups if you think the others would like to join you.'

'That sounds fine.'

'Bay! You're back!' The exclamation of delight sprang unchecked from her lips.

'I got in late yesterday afternoon,' he acknowledged. 'I thought I might see you here today with your father. I never guessed he would make you a galley-slave.'

Sabrina smiled at the teasing voice. 'Did you have a good trip?'

'Yes. I had some investment property to check on and inspected some other land I've been interested in acquiring. I even ran into an old friend I went to university with. He's topside talking to your father. Why don't you come and meet him?'

She had half expected it to be a woman, and she wondered if her relief was reflected in her expression. She hoped not. She didn't want Bay to think she was jealous. They were only friends.

'I'll be through here in a minute,' she said. 'If you'd like, you can take the coffeepot on up. There are some mugs in the cupboard. I can bring the sugar and powdered cream.'

'All right,' Bay agreed.

A few minutes later, Sabrina joined the others on deck. The wind lifted her bangs and she turned her face into the cooling flow of air.

'Here, Sabrina, let me take those.' Her father took the tins of sugar and powdered cream from her hands and helped her on deck.

'This is Grant's daughter, Sabrina Lane,' Bay said. 'This is my old fraternity brother, Doctor Joe Browning.'

'You'd better watch who you call old,' said a gruff male voice in a mock serious tone. Then Sabrina's hand was taken in greeting. 'I'm more commonly known as Joe or Doctor Joe to my patients.'

Cold fingers raced icily down her spine. 'How do you do.' Her greeting was stiff. Since her accident and the string of doctors she had been to, Sabrina had developed an aversion to those in the medical profession.

'Joe, the name is Joe,' he said. 'Your father tells me you've been blind for only a year. You seem to be getting along rather well.'

'There really isn't much choice, is there?' she retorted.

'Of course there is. You could always get along badly.'

His nonsensical reply unwillingly brought a faint smile to her mouth. She had always expected that even at home doctors were somewhat staid and unemotional, spouting platitudes and doing charitable deeds. This one seemed to be different.

'I ran into my share of furniture and buildings in the beginning,' she admitted.

'Do you use a cane or do you have a seeing eye dog?' He didn't give her a chance to reply. 'I hear they're using standard poodles as well as shepherds and other breeds as seeing eye dogs. Can you imagine a poodle prancing down the street with its fluffy pompadour and that ball of fluff on his tail leading some blind man? It always seemed like the height of absurdity to me. Not that I have anything against the intelligence of poodles.'

Sabrina laughed at the image he had created in her mind. She liked his irreverent attitude and her wariness disappeared. The relaxed sound of her laughter began a natural flow of conversation among all of them. Doctor Joe Browning dominated most of the topics with his dry wit.

Some time, Sabrina was not certain when, the subject became centered on her blindness, the accident, and the damage to her optic nerves that had resulted from the head injury. She was suddenly aware that the inquiries were not casual but had a professional undertone.

'Wait a minute,' she interrupted the doctor in mid-sentence. 'Exactly what kind of a doctor are you?'

'A very good one,' he quipped. 'A surgeon, to be specific.'

'What kind?' Then she raised her hand in a halting gesture, and accused angrily, 'No, let me guess. You're an eye surgeon.'

'You're right with the very first guess. Now that's the mark of a girl who pays attention,' Joe Browning replied without the least embarrassment.

'What have all these questions been? A subtle examination?'

'Yes,' he admitted simply.

Seething with indignation, Sabrina turned in the direction she knew Bay to be sitting. 'You put him up to this, didn't you, Bay Cameron? And you must have been in on it, too, Father.'

'It was my idea for you not to know the real reason why Doctor Joe was seeing you,' her father replied in a contrite tone. 'Bay did contact him originally, but the rest was my idea so you wouldn't have to go through the whole rigmarole again, maybe unnecessarily.'

'That's why you pretended,' Sabrina said tautly, 'that he was an old school chum of yours, isn't that right, Bay?'

'No, that's the truth,' the doctor replied, 'and it's also the truth that we bumped into each other in Los Angeles. He had no idea I was there since I've been on the East Coast for the last few years. He mentioned you to me and professional curiosity took over.'

'I'm sorry, Sabrina,' Bay offered quietly. 'I knew you'd be upset when you found out.'

'Then why did you try to trick me?'

'I felt I should respect your father's wishes. And there was the likelihood that you wouldn't find out, not if Joe didn't think there was any hope that your vision could be restored,' he answered.

'And do you?' Her chin tipped proudly toward the doctor. The aura of pride was a defence mechanism to conceal any reaction to his verdict.

'I'd like to run some more tests in a hospital before I give you a definite answer, Sabrina,' he said honestly. 'I would guess you have no more than a ten per cent chance, if that much, that there's a surgical cure.'

'Four specialists told my father and me that I would never see again. What makes you think you can help me?' Sabrina challenged.

'I don't know that I can,' Doctor Joe answered, 'but I don't know that I can't either. On occasions, the body's natural healing processes repair some of the damage, making a condition that was inoperable shortly after the injury operable a period of months later. It has happened.'

'I see,' she said tautly. 'And that's what you think has happened to me.'

'I don't know, but I don't think we should overlook the possibility,' he replied. 'To be certain, I'd have to admit you to a hospital and run some tests. I don't want to raise any false hopes, Sabrina. You have a

Janet Dailey

very slim chance of having your vision restored, right next to none at all. The decision is yours.'

Not even the scent of roses that her father had brought could overcome the strong medicinal and antiseptic odor of the hospital. In the corridor, there were the hushed voices of a pair of nurses walking swiftly by her door. Sabrina listened to the even breathing of the female patient who shared her room.

Visiting hours were over. The lights were out. She knew that because she had heard the flick of the switch when the nurse left the room a few minutes ago.

Her dark world seemed blacker this night. She felt so very much alone and vulnerable. She was afraid to hope that the tests tomorrow would be encouraging. Yet it was impossible to be indifferent to the reasons she was here.

A hand doubled into a fist at her side. Damn Bay for running into his doctor friend, Sabrina thought dejectedly. She had accepted her blindness, stopped fighting the injustice of it and had started living with it.

Since Bay was partially responsible for her presence in the hospital, the least he could have done was come to visit her. But no, he had sent a message of good luck with Doctor Joe, passed on when Sabrina had been admitted.

A trembling shivered over her body and wouldn't stop. She hadn't realized she was so scared. Her chin quivered. She wanted to break down and cry. The brave front she had worn was crumbling and she didn't care.

A swirl of air blew over her face. She had come to recognize that as the silent opening of the door to her hospital room. Someone was approaching her bed, and she had the sensation that it wasn't the nurse. A spicy scent of aftershave lotion drifting to her nose confirmed it.

'Are you awake?' Bay asked softly.

'Yes,' Sabrina whispered, pushing herself into a more upright position while trying to keep the flimsy hospital gown securely around her. 'Visiting hours are over. You're not supposed to be here.'

'If they catch me, they can ask me to leave, right?' he smiled with his voice. 'How are you doing?'

'Fine,' she lied. The edge of the bed took his weight. 'I thought Doctor Joe said you had to go to a party or something.'

'I did go,' Bay acknowledged, 'but I slipped away to see you. Is that all right?'

'It's all right with me as long as it was all right with the lady you were with,' Sabrina returned.

'What makes you think I was with anyone?'

'I certainly hope you were, because otherwise you're wearing some very expensive French perfume!' Her fingers clutched the bedcovers tightly. It was important that she maintain this air of lighthearted teasing so Bay would not guess her inner apprehension.

'Aha, the blind detective,' he mocked.

'Elementary,' she shrugged. 'After all, you were at a party. That makes it only logical to assume that you would turn your charm toward some attractive woman there.'

'Now that's where you're wrong.'

'Why?' Sabrina tilted her head to the side in mock challenge.

'Because I've been directing all my charms to a certain blind lady that I know, a very attractive one,' Bay responded lightly.

Her throat constricted. 'I find that difficult to believe.'

A hand warmly covered the hands clinging to the sheets. Gently he prised them free. 'Your hands are like ice, Sabrina. What's the matter?'

His frowning accusation set an uncontrollable shiver quaking over her shoulders. Emitting a shaky sigh, Sabrina admitted, 'I'm frightened, Bay — of tomorrow.'

He said nothing for a minute. She felt him shift his weight on the bed. Then his arm circled her shoulders and he drew her against his chest, the back of his hand cradling her head near his chin.

'Let's think about this,' he murmured calmly. 'It's not the thought of the tests Joe is going to do that frightens you. That only leaves two alternatives. One is that you're afraid to have your sight restored and the second is that you won't, right?'

Numbly Sabrina nodded her affirmation. The steady beat of his heart beneath her head and the protective circle of his strong arms was blissfully comforting.

'I know you can't be afraid of seeing again,' he continued. 'That result would have everyone rejoicing. That only leaves the second.'

'I —' she began hesitantly. 'I had accepted the fact that I was blind. I've started working in clay, did I tell you that? I'm an awful coward,' she sighed. 'I wish I'd never agreed to these tests. I wish I'd never met

Doctor Joe. I don't want to go through the agony of accepting all over again that I'm permanently blind.'

'Where is that gutsy girl who was always trying to thumb her nose at convention?' Bay mocked softly. 'You aren't a coward, Sabrina. A coward wouldn't be here in the hospital taking the slim gamble that Joe offered. If the tests prove negative, you aren't going to wail and pound your chest. The gutsy girl I know is going to shrug her shoulders and say, "Well, I gave it a go." ' She felt him smile against her hair. 'To borrow an old cliché, Sabrina, you have everything to gain and nothing to lose.'

'That's what I keep trying to tell myself,' she sighed.

'The secret is to stop saying and start admitting that it's true.' He didn't require a reply as he held her for more long minutes. The strength seemed to flow from the muscles in his arms into her, chasing away her unreasonable fears. 'Are you all right now?' he asked finally.

'Yes,' she nodded against his chin, and smiled faintly.

'Then I'd better be going before the nurse comes in and gets the wrong idea about what we're doing,' Bay teased softly.

Very gently he shifted her on to the pillow, tucking the sheet around her chest. As he started to straighten, Sabrina reached out for his arm.

'Thank you for coming, Bay,' she whispered tightly.

'Don't thank me for something I wanted to do.' Then he bent over her and there was a tantalizing brush of his mouth on hers. 'Goodnight, Sabrina. I'll be seeing you.'

'Yes. Goodnight Bay.'

There were soft footsteps, then the swish of air as the door opened and closed.

The hospital bed felt like a pincushion. Sabrina knew it was the waiting. Two days of tests were over, and Doctor Joe would be relaying the results any minute. The grimness that had been in his voice the last day had convinced Sabrina that the results thus far hadn't been encouraging.

Her father walked again to the window in her room. She knew he had no interest in the parking lot below, his patience giving way to restless pacing. She wished she could join him. In almost mid-stride he stopped and turned abruptly. A second later air from the corridor fanned her cheek and she turned toward the door.

'Good morning, Sabrina, Mr. Lane,' Doctor Joe Browning greeted each of them. His voice was professionally bright. 'It's really a lousy morning, but I suppose you San Franciscans are used to the fog.'

'Good morning, Doctor Joe,' Sabrina returned.

But her father skipped the pleasantries. 'Are all the results in?'

'Yes.'

The back of Sabrina's neck prickled. Unconsciously she called out hesitantly, 'Bay?'

'Hello, Sabrina,' he answered quietly.

'Don't tell me my patient has mental telepathy?' the doctor laughed shortly in surprise.

'A keen sense of smell,' Bay corrected in a smiling voice. 'She probably recognized my aftershave lotion.'

Sabrina didn't correct him. She wasn't certain herself how she had known he was there, and she couldn't be positive that she hadn't unconsciously caught a whiff of the spicy fragrance.

'Well, to get back to the business at hand,' Doctor Joe breathed in deeply, 'I've analyzed the test results twice.'

He paused and Grant Lane prompted, 'And?'

'We knew when we rolled the dice, Mr. Lane, that it was a long shot, not even house odds.' The grimness of his voice was all the warning Sabrina needed to brace herself for the rest of his answer. 'The dice came up snake eyes. There isn't anything that can be done. I'm deeply sorry that I put both of you through this.'

The silence from her father told Sabrina how much he had been praying for a miracle. So had she, for that matter, but she wasn't as crushed as she had been the other times that the verdict was pronounced.

She summoned a weak smile. 'We had to take the chance, Doctor Joe.' Her smile deepened as she remembered Bay's words that first night in the hospital. 'We had to give it a go.'

The doctor walked to the bed and clasped one of her hands warmly between his. 'Thank you, Sabrina.'

As Doctor Joe took his leave of her father, apologizing again, she heard Bay approach the bed. He stopped somewhere near the side. She felt his penetrating gaze run over her face.

'Are you all right?' he asked quietly.

'Yes,' she whispered, and she knew suddenly that it was the truth and not simply brave words.

'I knew that gutsy blind queen would resurface,' he told her.

'With your help, she did,' Sabrina answered.

'I can't take the credit for the strength you already possessed,' Bay denied, 'but we'll argue the point another time. How about Saturday night?'

'Saturday night?' she repeated.

'Yes, we can have dinner together. I'll pick you up around seven.'

There was a breathless catch in her throat. 'Is that an order or an invitation?' she asked unevenly.

'Both, depending on your answer.'

'I'd be proud to have dinner with you, Mr. Cameron,' Sabrina accepted with a demure inclination of her head.

More than proud, she added silently to herself. She found she was looking forward to Saturday night with uncommon eagerness.

Six

Sabrina slowly descended the steps to the second floor, fingering the soft knit of her top uncertainly. A tiny frown of indecision pulled the arch of her brows together. In the living room, she could hear her father's and Deborah's voices. She walked to the open doorway and paused.

'Deborah, may I see you a minute?' Sabrina requested, a hint of anxiety in her voice.

'Of course.' Footsteps muffled by the carpet quickly approached the doorway where she waited. 'What is it?'

'This pant suit, is it too dressy?'

'I shouldn't think so,' Deborah frowned in confusion. 'Bay is taking you out to dinner, isn't he?'

'Not to dinner exactly,' Sabrina explained. 'We'll pick up something to eat at the Wharf like we did the last time and have a makeshift picnic somewhere. He's not taking me out to a public restaurant.' Her hand touched the camel tan slacks stitched in dark brown and the matching boat-necked top in the same brown. Over her arm, she carried a matching jacket and around her neck were progressively longer strands of gold chain. 'Maybe I should wear something simpler?'

'I don't think so,' Deborah decided after several seconds of consideration to the question. 'You may not be going out to a fancy restaurant to dine, but that isn't any reason why you have to look like an urchin. That pant suit is versatile enough to fit any occasion except the most formal one.'

'Good,' Sabrina sighed in relief. It was so difficult sometimes trying to judge by memory the clothes she wore. The front door bell rang. 'That must be Bay now.'

'Your purse is on the table,' Deborah stated. 'I'll tell Bay you're on your way down.'

Retrieving her purse, Sabrina slipped the ivory cane from the umbrella stand, hooked it over her arm and opened the stairwell door, calling a goodbye to her father before closing it. She darted eagerly down the stairs and through the street door to the gates.

'I'm ready,' she declared unnecessarily, unlocking the gates and walking through.

Bay's hand touched her arm in light possession as he directed her to his parked car. 'I was hoping you might wear that new dress tonight.'

Sabrina laughed softly. 'I'd look pretty silly wearing that to a picnic!'

'A picnic?' he repeated. 'We aren't going to a picnic. I'm taking you out to dinner, remember?'

'But —' she stopped short.

'But what?' He paused patiently beside her.

'You know very well that I don't eat in public places,' she stated, punctuating the sentence with an emphatic tap of her cane.

'Yes, I remember what you said.' His arm crossed her back and he forcibly moved her toward the car. The door was opened and Sabrina was helped and shoved inside. She fumbled for the door handle, only to find the door was locked. Before she could find the lock, Bay was in the car, his hand tightly closing over her wrist.

'You're not paying attention to me,' Sabrina accused.

'I can't give you all of my attention and drive too,' Bay countered logically, starting the car and turning it away from the curb with one hand. 'We're going to a nice little Italian restaurant. It doesn't look much from the outside, but the food is excellent.'

'I'm not going,' she declared.

'Sabrina, you can't keep avoiding things on the off chance that you'll do something embarrassing.' The firm tone of his voice said his patience was thinning.

'You're going to look pretty silly yourself dragging me into that restaurant,' she commented smugly.

'I hope you aren't counting on the fact that I won't, because if that's the only way I can get you in the door, I'll do it,' Bay stated.

In that flashing second, Sabrina realized that he meant it. No stubbornness or anger on her part would change his mind. He actually meant to get her in the restaurant one way or the other.

'You're a brute and a bully!' she hissed angrily. 'I don't know why I ever agreed to come with you tonight. I should have guessed you would do something like this.'

'You'd better be careful,' he warned mockingly. 'I could change my mind and take you to a Chinese restaurant and put a pair of chopsticks in your hand. I don't think you'd fare too successfully with those.'

The pouting line of her mouth twitched as her innate sense of humor surfaced. She covered her mouth with her hand to try to hide the smile that was breaking through. She had never mastered the use of chopsticks when she could see. Any attempt now that she was blind would be absurd.

'I see that smile,' Bay laughed softly. 'It's a decided improvement on that stubborn blind monkey that was sitting beside me a minute ago. You just keep wearing it. And don't be embarrassed if you spill something. Sighted people do it all the time.'

'Why can't I ever win an argument with you?' Sabrina sighed, but with humor.

'Because, my little blind queen,' he drawled, 'you always know that I'm right.'

Surprisingly, as far as Sabrina was concerned, the dinner was without mishap. The other times she had eaten out shortly after the accident, she had invariably tipped over a glass or dropped food on the table, but not this time. Bay had laughingly threatened to order her spaghetti, but it was a very excellent lasagna that she had received instead.

She leaned back in her chair, a hand securely touching the coffee cup so she wouldn't forget where it was. A tiny sigh of contentment broke from her lips.

'What was that for?' Bay inquired softly.

'For a very enjoyable meal,' she responded. 'Thank you for making me come.'

'I prefer the word "persuaded." ' Amusement danced in his voice.

'"Persuaded" me to come then,' she acknowledged with a dimpling smile.

'No depression because of the negative test results?' Despite the teasing tone, there was an underlying hint of seriousness.

'I wish it had been otherwise, of course,' Sabrina shrugged, 'but I don't mind as much as I might have. Partly because of the advice you gave me and partly because I'd already started working again, in a creative sense. My life as a blind woman was not without purpose when I went into the hospital this time. Before when the specialists gave me their verdict, I had nothing to look forward to but emptiness. Now, I have a goal.'

'You're referring to the modeling you've started in clay. When are you going to show me what you've done so far?'

'When I'm willing to stand some criticism,' Sabrina smiled ruefully.

'And you think my judgment would be critical?' Bay prompted.

'I don't think you're going to let me get by with mediocrity simply because I'm blind,' she acknowledged.

'I don't think you would lean on that crutch and lower your standards either,' he returned.

'I couldn't,' admitted Sabrina with a nod of her head. A fervent note crept into her voice. 'I want to be more than just good. I want to be great. It's the only way I'll be able to support myself with art as my career.'

'And that's very important to you, isn't it?'

'Yes. Not just for pride's sake or to be independent,' she went on earnestly, 'but because I don't want to keep being a burden to my father. I know he doesn't think of me that way, but I know that because of me he hasn't married Deborah. Only by having an independent income could I prove to him that I'm capable of living on my own.'

'You could always get married. That's a very excellent reason for leaving home,' Bay suggested.

'There happen to be two obstacles to that solution,' Sabrina laughed shortly, not taking his suggestion seriously.

'What are they?'

'First, there isn't anyone I happen to be in love with, and it would be pretty shallow to marry a man simply to get out of the house.'

'And the second?'

'The second is a very crucial one. There would have to be someone around willing to marry me.' There was a dubious shake of her head as if such a contingency would never occur.

'Is that so unlikely?' Bay asked with curious mockery.

'If they're sane, it would be.' She laughed quietly again.

'I've always considered myself to be sane. I guess that puts me out of the running, doesn't it?'

Sabrina felt his gaze searching her face, alert to her reaction. She was suddenly self-conscious about the subject they were discussing.

'It certainly would,' she answered firmly.

'I guess that settles that,' Bay stated. The nonchalance in his voice didn't match the sensation Sabrina had that he had been interested in her answer. Maybe he thought she wanted to take advantage of his apparent wealth. 'Would you like some more coffee, Sabrina, or shall we leave?'

'No more, thank you. I'm ready if you are.' Her hand found the ivory cane hooked over the arm of her chair.

After that first successful dinner, Bay took Sabrina out several times during the following weeks. The restaurants he chose were seldom crowded but served excellent food.

The only twinges of self-consciousness she experienced came when friends of Bay's stopped at their table to say hello. She had sensed their surprise upon learning she was blind and guessed that they wondered why Bay was with her.

At odd times, she wondered why herself, but the answer had ceased to be important. It was enough to enjoy his company without constantly questioning his motives for being with her. In a way she didn't want to find out. She was afraid his reason might be a charitable one. Although she had come a great distance out of her shell, she was still averse to pity from any quarter and most especially from Bay.

Carefully she smoothed the arm of the clay figure, letting her fingers transfer the image to her mind's eye. A faint shiver of subdued elation trembled over her at the completed picture of a ballet dancer captured in the middle of a pirouette that her mind saw. With each passing week her hands had become more sure and more adept. The successes had begun to outnumber the failures.

Footsteps echoed into the studio from the stairway. Quelling her excitement, Sabrina stepped back from the work stand, a faint smile of triumph tickling the corners of her mouth. Wiping her hands on the towel, she turned slightly toward the door as the footsteps approached. An eagerness she couldn't conceal was in her stance.

'Come in, Dad,' she called when the footsteps paused at the door. 'I've finished the third. Come and see it.'

The instant the door opened, her head tipped sideways in a listening attitude. The person entering the room was not her father but Bay. She knew it instinctively.

'What are you doing here?' she breathed in surprise 'You said you wouldn't come until seven. It can't be that late.' She had removed her watch so she couldn't check the time.

'It isn't. It's the middle of the afternoon,' Bay returned with faint amusement. 'Since you haven't extended an invitation for me to see your work, I persuaded your father to send me up here rather than have you come down.'

In an instinctive, protective movement, Sabrina moved a few steps to try to block his line of sight. Only her father and Deborah had seen the result of her many hours of labor in the studio. She was not yet ready for someone outside her family to see what she had done.

'That doesn't explain what you're doing here in the middle of the afternoon,' she murmured defensively.

'Doesn't it? I thought it did.' She could hear the smile in his tone. 'Actually you're right,' Bay conceded. 'I had another purpose for coming other than sneaking into your studio. I'm afraid I have to cancel our dinner date tonight — I'm sorry, Sabrina.'

'That's all right,' she shrugged.

It wasn't all right, but she didn't want him to realize how much she looked forward to an evening with him. She didn't like to admit it to herself. There was no future in it. The future was here in this studio with her work.

'I don't know whether I should be pleased or insulted that you've taken the news so calmly.' Sabrina sensed the arching of a thick brow in her direction, faintly mocking and faintly curious. 'You might show a little regret.'

'I would have enjoyed the evening.' Pride inserted a slightly indifferent tone in her voice. 'Obviously whatever it is that's forced you to cancel our dinner together must be important or I don't think you would have canceled.' The intense scrutiny of his gaze was disturbing. Striving for lightness, Sabrina added with a taut smile, 'I certainly hope you've warned your jealous girlfriend that she doesn't need to scratch my eyes out. I'm already quite blind and disfigurement I don't need.' It was a facetious remark, not an expression of self-pity.

'What makes you think it's a jealous girlfriend who's changing our plans?' The inflection in his voice was mockingly amused, but Sabrina was still conscious of his penetrating look.

'I don't know that it is,' she answered with a teasing smile. 'But I certainly hope you don't expect me to believe that you're a celibate.'

'What makes you think I'm not?' Bay countered.

The virilely masculine face her hands had seen was immediately before her inner eye. The image made a mockery of his question. In too many little ways, Bay's actions in the past had answered his own question.

'A girl has ways of knowing these things,' Sabrina smiled complacently. 'A kind of female intuition, I suppose.'

'If you believe that about me, then what conclusion have you reached to explain why I haven't brought our relationship to a more intimate level?' he asked lazily.

'Really, Bay!' Sabrina laughed as if the question was ridiculous under the circumstances. 'We're friends, nothing more.'

'Strictly platonic, is that it?'

'Of course.' A tiny frown puckered her forehead at the faint harshness in his remark.

'In that case, when are you going to step aside to let a "friend" see your work? My view is somewhat limited with you standing in front of it,' he mocked.

Sabrina decided that she had imagined the sharpness in his previous question. She had only been stating the obvious and he had agreed in an indirect way.

For a hesitant moment, she remained where she was, wanting to know his reaction to her work but unsure yet of the extent of her own skill in this field of art. Almost reluctantly she stepped to one side, apprehension edging the corners of her bland expression as Bay walked forward for a closer look.

'S-some of my first attempts are on the side table,' she explained nervously. 'As you can see, they aren't very good, but I've slowly been improving. Right now I'm working on a series of ballet figures. I thought I'd do a small "corps de ballet" with the central model being a dancing couple. I'm only a third done with the secondary figures, though.'

The silence stretched seemingly without end. Sabrina thought she would burst with the suspense of waiting. Her hands were unconsciously clasped in a praying position.

'Have any of your friends seen your work?' Bay asked absently. 'Your art friends, I mean.'

Her throat worked convulsively as she shook her head in a negative answer before she could speak. 'Only Dad and Deborah.'

'I'm no critic, Sabrina,' he murmured. 'I only know what I like, and I'm impressed by what I see here. You've never done any extensive work in this medium before?'

'Never,' she breathed. 'Do you really think it's good? You're not saying it because I'm blind, are you?' She needed to hear his approval again.

'I haven't treated you with kid gloves since the first time I met you, and I'm not going to put them on now,' he answered seriously. 'You know that what you've done is more than good. I can see that it is. A professional is the only person who can tell you how good you are. If you want my suggestion, I think you should get hold of someone who can give you that answer.'

'Not — not yet,' Sabrina refused. Confidence in her own ability was not to the point where she could endure the scrutiny of her work by an art critic. 'I'm not ready for that. I need more time.'

'No one is ever ready to have anything judged by others, but you can't postpone it for ever.' His observance was gently understanding while reminding her of the practical need if she intended to make this her career.

'Not yet,' she repeated, running her palms nervously over the sides of her clay-stained smock.

'Cigarette?' Bay offered.

'Yes, please.' Sabrina accepted with a quaking sigh.

As the scent of burning tobacco reached her nose, she extended her hand for the cigarette, but Bay placed the filter tip against her lips, his fingers touching her mouth and sending a shiver of awareness down her spine. Invariably when she came in contact with him, she was intensely conscious of his maleness, the memory of that one fleeting first kiss haunting her again with its tender mastery and checked fire.

'There's coffee and cake downstairs,' she offered hesitantly. 'If you'd —'

'No, I'm sorry, I can't stay any longer,' Bay refused before she could complete the invitation. 'I won't be able to see you this coming week either. I do have a couple of tickets for the Light Opera's performance next Saturday if you're willing to accept that as a raincheck for tonight.'

'I would enjoy that,' Sabrina smiled.

'I promise I'll make certain I don't have to cancel that one,' he smiled. 'Oh, by the way, there's something I meant to give you as an apology for tonight.'

'Give me?' she frowned as she listened to him reach into his pocket and heard the faint rustle of paper. He placed a small, wrapped box in her hand, long and thin, similar in shape to a jeweler's box.

'Open it,' he ordered, laughing at her hesitation. 'It's nothing expensive, if that's what's concerning you. In fact, you might decide to throw it in my face when you find out what it is.'

Curious and apprehensive, Sabrina began unwrapping the package. Removing the cardboard top of the small, thin box, her exploring fingers touched a pair of tapering sticks. She turned a bewildered expression to Bay.

'Sticks?' she questioned in disbelief.

Bay clicked his tongue in mock reproval. 'Not just sticks,' he chuckled. 'They're chopsticks. I'm giving you a couple of weeks to practise before I take you to a Cantonese restaurant in Chinatown.'

Laughter bubbled in her throat and she bit into her lower lip to hold it back. With mock seriousness she replied, 'I suppose I should be grateful that you've given me advance warning.'

'Yes, you should,' he agreed in a tone of pseudo-arrogance.

'Even with practice,' Sabrina couldn't hold back the laughter, 'the only thing I'll probably eat is egg rolls, soup and fortune cookies. All the rest will end up on the floor or the table cloth.'

'I'll take the chance,' Bay smiled. 'As for next Saturday, I think the occasion will warrant the sophistication of that flame-colored dress.'

'Is that an order, too?' she laughed.

'If it is, will you obey it?' he countered.

'Yes,' she nodded, a wide smile spreading across her cheeks, softening her square jawline.

After Bay's approval of her work, Sabrina strove even harder for the perfection she demanded. This renewed vigor made the week pass swiftly. The performance of the Light Opera Company the following Saturday seemed a reward for her efforts.

The faint initial nervousness she had felt at the prospect of going to such a very public place vanished under the genuine praise from Bay at her appearance. She had taken extra pains, enlisting Deborah's aid with her hair and make-up. The two of them had got along much better since Sabrina had started working in the studio again.

No further mention had been made by Deborah of the special school she had thought Sabrina should attend. It was as if they were both counting on the efforts in the studio for the future happiness of each.

Sabrina had not intended to take her ivory cane, vanity not wanting her to be easily identified by the crowd attending the opera as being blind. However, Bay handed her the cane from the umbrella stand as they walked out the door of the house. She had known he would chide her reason for not wanting to carry it, so she had said nothing.

Now the cane was hooked over her arm as they stood in the foyer of the theater. It was intermission between acts. Had Sabrina been with anyone else she would probably have remained in her seat, but Bay had ushered her into the outer lobby.

Bay Cameron was not a man to be overlooked by those around him. His very stature would draw attention to him even if his male magnetism didn't. Thus Sabrina knew she was the object of many people's interest and curiosity, especially once they saw the cane on her arm, because she was in his company.

Several people acquainted with Bay stopped, politely including her in their greeting. Bay did not encourage conversation with anyone and they gradually drifted away after the initial exchange. Sabrina wasn't certain whether it was because he was aware of her uneasiness with strangers or because he was self-conscious that she was blind. The last didn't seem to fit with his nature and she dismissed it.

'Bay Cameron!' an older woman greeted him effusively. Unconsciously Sabrina edged closer to be nearer his protection. 'I haven't seen you in ages!' the woman exclaimed. 'Where have you been keeping yourself? Is this the little lady I have to blame for your absence?'

His hand moved to rest on the back of Sabrina's shoulders, drawing her slightly forward as he introduced her. 'Pamela, I'd like you to meet Sabrina Lane. Sabrina, this is a very dear friend of mine, Pamela

Thyssen. She tends to be a bit overpowering and nosy, but she has a gentle heart.'

'Don't you believe him!' the woman commanded gruffly, a raspy edge to her otherwise cultured voice. 'My bite is every bit as bad as my bark, so beware, Miss Lane. It is "Miss" Lane, isn't it?'

'Do you see what I mean, Sabrina?' Bay chuckled. 'She's a nosy busybody.'

'Yes, it is Miss Lane,' Sabrina confirmed with a faint smile.

She was beginning to agree that Bay's description of Pamela Thyssen was correct. Although curious and forceful, underneath the woman seemed to be kind.

'We single women must stick together,' Pamela Thyssen averred. 'Not that I intend to remain single. I've outlived two husbands, and they always say the third is a charm. And you, my dear, are you setting your cap for our Bay?'

Sabrina flushed deeply. 'Hardly, Mrs. Thyssen,' she denied vigorously.

'I guess that puts you in your place, Bay!' the woman laughed loudly.

'She's a very independent young lady,' he agreed with faint amusement, yet she sensed an inner displeasure in his tone.

'I must get to know Sabrina better. Bring her to my party after the performance.' It was a command, not a request, and the older woman bade them goodbye before Sabrina could prompt Bay into a refusal.

'You aren't actually intending to go, are you?' she said in a half-demand when they were alone.

'Why not?' he countered smoothly. 'Pamela's parties are quiet ones and friendly.'

'I'm uncomfortable with a lot of strangers,' Sabrina answered defensively.

'It's about time you got over that,' Bay responded, the hand on her back prodding her into movement. 'Now we only have a few minutes to find our seats before the curtain goes up.'

Seven

Sabrina curled her fingers into the soft rabbit fur of her black evening jacket, pushing the collar around her neck. The corners of her mouth drooped downward in frustration as she nibbled at her sensitive lower lip. The closed window of the car did not completely block out the sound of other cars exiting the theater lot.

'Why can't you take me home and go to the party by yourself?' The suggestion she made had a vaguely desperate ring to it.

'The invitation was for both of us,' Bay reminded her.

'Mrs. Thyssen doesn't know me. She wouldn't even miss me if I wasn't there,' Sabrina reasoned.

'Yes, she will.' A smile lightened the firmness of his tone. 'Especially since you were the one who prompted her to extend the invitation.'

'I did no such thing!'

'Let me rephrase it,' he said patiently. 'It was after meeting you and having her curiosity aroused that she invited us to her party.'

'She never gave us a chance to say whether we could come or not. We could have made other plans for all she knows,' Sabrina argued.

'But we don't have other plans, do we? There isn't any reason why we can't go to her party for a short while.'

'I don't want to go. That's a good enough reason for me.' Her chin jutted out defiantly.

'No, it isn't,' Bay replied in a voice that said he would not be swayed by any more arguments.

'You're a bully, Bay Cameron!' Sabrina accused lowly, slumping in her seat.

'A gentle one, I hope,' he chuckled softly.

'A bully,' she repeated with no qualifying adjectives.

76

Bridling at the way Bay had maneuvered her again into a situation not of her choosing, Sabrina couldn't concentrate on the direction they were taking. She lost track of the turns and eventually stopped guessing what streets they were on. The absence of any heavy traffic indicated a residential area, but she had no idea what section of the city they were in.

The car slowed down and turned into the curb. 'Here we are,' Bay announced, switching off the motor and opening the door.

Sabrina said nothing, sitting in mutinous silence as the door opened and closed on his side. In her mind, she watched him walk around the car to her door, judging almost to the second when he opened her door. Stubbornly she didn't move.

'Are you coming in with me or are you going to sit in the car and sulk like a little child?' Bay mocked softly.

'If I have a choice, I'll stay in the car,' she declared coldly.

'Sabrina.' His sighing voice held indulgent patience in its gentle tone. 'Are you really going to let some strangers intimidate you into staying in the car?'

'They don't intimidate me.'

'You're afraid to go in. What other word fits?'

'I'm not afraid,' Sabrina asserted forcefully.

'Of course not,' Bay agreed in a deliberately disbelieving voice.

'I'm not!' she repeated angrily.

'Whatever you say,' he agreed again with the same inflection. 'If you're going to stay in the car, I suggest you lock all the doors. I'll be gone about an hour.'

'You're not really leaving me here?' Sabrina frowned, tipping her head back, not certain any more if he was teasing or serious.

'You said you'd rather stay in the car,' Bay reminded her complacently. 'I'll put in my appearance and explain why you couldn't come.'

'You wouldn't dare tell Mrs. Thyssen that I'm sitting out here in the car?' she breathed. But her question was only met with silence, a silence that held an affirmative answer. 'You're completely without scruples,' she grumbled, turning to slide her feet out of the car, his hand reaching out for her arm to guide her safely to the sidewalk.

A maid admitted them into the house. The sound of warm, friendly voices filled the foyer entrance. It seemed to come from several directions, indicating that the party was larger than the small gathering that had been Sabrina's impression.

With her evening jacket in the maid's possession, Bay took her arm and led her in the direction where the majority of voices seemed to be coming from. Her mouth tightened in a grim line.

'Smile.' Bay's order was whispered near her ear.

'No.' But the severe displeasure of her expression lessened.

Sabrina was unaware of the faintly regal tilt of her head, accenting the swanlike column of her neck as they entered the room. Her queenly posture and the softly molding flame-colored gown drew as much attention to her as was given to Bay. Since he was acquainted with most of the people there, the expressions of greeting were offered to him.

Stubbornly Sabrina didn't acknowledge any of them. Only the white knuckles of the hand clutching the ivory cane revealed the inner tremblings she felt at being in a roomful of strangers.

From their right, the instantly recognizable voice of Mrs. Pamela Thyssen called out to them. 'Bay — Sabrina! I'm so glad you could come.'

Sabrina's greeting when the woman was beside them consisted of only a polite 'hello.' She did not intend to lie by saying that she was glad to be there.

Bracelets jangled from the older woman's wrist. The hand that grasped Sabrina's free hand was heavy with rings, small and large. Her perfume was a comfortable, old-fashioned scent of violets.

'Bay, be a dear,' Pamela Thyssen commanded. 'Go and fetch Sabrina and me a drink. I'll take my usual and bring Sabrina the same.'

'Really, Mrs. Thyssen,' Sabrina started her protest, but Bay had already moved away from her side, 'I don't care for anything to drink.'

'Neither do I. My usual happens to be iced tea,' the woman murmured in a confidential aside. 'That's a little secret between you and me. A hostess is expected to drink at her own parties or the guests don't feel free to imbibe. Iced tea looks sufficiently like drink to make the others feel at ease. So relax, my dear, I shan't attempt to free your tongue with intoxicating beverages.'

'I doubt if you could,' Sabrina answered almost beneath her breath.

'You have spirit. I like that,' Pamela pronounced. 'I'm Bay's godmother. Did he tell you?'

'No.' Was that the reason for the woman's apparent curiosity about her, Sabrina wondered to herself.

'His parents are in Europe on a second honeymoon. Louise, that's Bay's mother, and I grew up together. We've always been very close friends.'

'He mentioned they were in Europe,' she confirmed, since there seemed little other comment she could offer.

'I've been admiring your cane. It is ivory, isn't it?' There was no pause for a reply. 'It's a beautiful piece of workmanship, and so elegant as well. Where did you ever find it?'

'It was a gift — from a friend,' Sabrina added after a second's hesitation. Bay could tell the woman himself if he wanted her to know it was from him.

'A special friend?' the woman queried in a prompting way.

'A friend,' was the only explanation Sabrina offered.

'How long have you been blind, Sabrina?'

'Almost a year.' Her chin lifted fractionally as if to say she did not want any probing questions into her past.

'And how long have you known Bay?'

'About two months. Mrs. Thyssen —' Sabrina began, taking a deep breath in the hopes of switching the conversation to some other topic less personal, hopefully without offending the other woman.

'Speak of the devil,' Pamela Thyssen murmured, cutting her off in midsentence. 'That didn't take you very long, Bay. Thank you.'

The clink of rings against a glass accompanied the words. In the next instant, Bay's voice said, 'Here you are, Sabrina,' and a cold glass was placed in her outstretched hand. 'How have you two been getting along while I've been gone? I see by the queenly tilt of Sabrina's nose that you must have been prying already, Pamela.'

'Not prying, Bay,' Pamela corrected with a laugh. 'I was merely trying to find out more about her.' In absent musing, she added, 'She does have a queenly air about her, doesn't she?'

'Please, I —' Sabrina started another protest, but it wasn't allowed to be completed either.

'— don't like to be talked about as if you weren't here,' Pamela Thyssen finished the sentence. 'I know very well what you mean and despise it myself. But it was meant as a compliment. Sabrina and I don't need a referee, Bay. Why don't you go and circulate or something? Let me have her for an hour. I'll take care of her.'

Sabrina turned in Bay's direction, her lips parting in a silent plea for him not to desert her. For a fleeting second she thought he was going to debate the other woman's request.

'You're in good hands, Sabrina,' he said quietly. 'Pamela won't let you fall. I'll see you later on.'

The line of her mouth thinned angrily as he moved away. First he maneuvered her into coming to this party attended by strangers, then he deserted her! Irritation seethed beneath the surface at her inability to escape from the situation on her own. Independence could only be attained to a certain point, after that she was at the mercy of those around her.

'Come, my dear,' Pamela Thyssen hooked her arm in Sabrina's, 'I want to introduce you around. I try to choose my friends carefully, so with luck we'll avoid meeting any snobs.'

Gritting her teeth silently, Sabrina was practically forced to accompany her hostess. The following flurry of introductions and new voices were difficult to assimilate and put the correct name to the appropriate voice.

There was not one condescending remark or patronizing comment regarding her blindness. The main topic of conversation was the performance that evening. Several of the people she met had seen her at the theater and inquired about her opinion. Everyone's interest in her seemed to be friendly without pitying overtones. Gradually Sabrina's defensive attitude relaxed.

'Tommy, why don't you let Sabrina sit in that love-seat with Mrs. Phillips?' Pamela Thyssen suggested in the firmly ordering tone. 'The armrest is just to your left, dear.'

The glass of tea, empty now, was taken from her hand as the searching tip of her cane found the front edge of the small sofa. Willingly Sabrina sat down. The obstacle course of strange names and voices was beginning to tire her and she guessed that the astute Pamela Thyssen had sensed it. She conceded, but only to herself, that Bay had been right when he said he was leaving her in good hands.

'That's an absolutely stunning dress you're wearing, Miss Lane,' the woman at her side stated, obviously the Mrs. Phillips that Pamela had mentioned. 'I noticed it in the theater.'

The compliment was followed by the woman's lengthy dissertation on the difficulty she had finding clothes to fit her properly and how uncomplimentary the present styles were to her figure. Sabrina listened, inserting a monosyllabic answer when she thought one was required but letting the other woman carry the conversation.

The sensitive area on the back of her neck began to tingle. Sabrina instantly guessed the cause. Bay Cameron had to be somewhere near. Her radar was seldom wrong where he was concerned. Pretending a concentration on the woman speaking to her, she strained her hearing to catch any sound that might pinpoint his location.

Then came the husky caressing sound of a feminine voice, vaguely familiar although Sabrina couldn't place it. 'Bay darling, I didn't expect to see you here.'

'It's a surprise running into you, too,' she heard Bay answer calmly. 'I thought you didn't care for Pamela's parties. I thought they were much too tame for you.'

'A girl can change her mind, can't she, darling?' the voice purred.

'And a man can always wonder why?' Bay countered.

'Actually a little bird saw you at the theater tonight and passed the word on to me. I took a guess that you might bring your little sparrow to Pamela's party.'

'Did you?' was his noncommittal reply.

'I don't think I'll ever understand that streak of charity you possess, Bay,' the silky feminine voice said. 'I mean, why do you have to take such a personal interest in the poor girl? Why can't you simply give her a bunch of money and be done with her? You certainly can afford it.'

Sabrina stiffened. She couldn't help it. The only saving grace in the whole situation was that she doubted anyone possessed the acute hearing that blindness had given her and Bay's conversation with the woman wasn't being overheard by anyone but herself.

'Would that be your solution, Roni?' he murmured in a low voice. 'Sometimes I think when they were handing out compassion, you went back to the line marked "passion." '

Roni. That was the name of the girl who had been with him that one day at the Yacht Harbor. Sabrina also remembered that Bay had said they were going to take in an ocean sunset, a romantic offer if she had ever heard one.

'Is it so bad,' the woman named Roni was speaking again, 'to be passionate, Bay?' Her voice was a caressing whisper that Sabrina could barely understand.

'Not in certain situations.' He sounded amused, as if he was remembering times when he had not felt the need to criticize Roni's passion. Sabrina's blood started to boil, temper bubbling hotly to her nerve ends.

'Tell me, darling,' Sabrina had the impression that the girl moved closer to Bay in an intimately confiding manner, 'you aren't trying to use that blind girl to make me jealous. Isn't that just a little ridiculous?'

'Why? She's a very attractive girl,' Bay stated, without denying the charge.

'But she's blind,' Roni reminded him. 'I know you must feel sorry for her. We all feel pity for those less fortunate than ourselves, but how cruel it must be for the girl when she eventually discovers that all the attention you've been giving her is because of pity. I don't think she'll thank you.'

'Knowing Sabrina, she would probably slap my face if —' Bay drawled.

But Sabrina didn't listen to the rest of his statement. She had heard enough. Her stomach was twisted into knots of tortuous pain. A black nausea attacked her head, swirling in sickening circles as she rose to her feet, unmindful of Mrs. Phillips' continuing voice.

'Excuse me,' she interrupted sharply. 'Mrs. Thyssen?' Her questing voice searched for the location of her hostess somewhere nearby.

'Yes, Sabrina.' Pamela Thyssen was instantly at her side, a curious note in the voice that answered her summons.

Sabrina swallowed, trying to calm her screeching nerves and make her voice sound as natural as possible.

'Would you please direct me to your powder room?'

'Of course. It's this way. Come with me.' A ringed hand guided her from the small group. 'Are you all right, Sabrina?' Pamela Thyssen asked in a concerned tone. 'You look pale. Are you quite sure you're feeling all right?' her hostess repeated.

'Quite sure,' Sabrina forced a smile of assurance.

Free of much of the party, they turned into what Sabrina guessed was a hallway. Her nerves were raw. The voices in the other room seemed to take on a higher pitch. Although she tried desperately, she couldn't block her hearing.

'Here we are,' Pamela stated. 'The door is directly to your left.'

Sabrina stopped, letting her cane determine the distance to the door before she turned to her hostess. 'Thank you, Mrs. Thyssen.'

'Would you like me to go in with you?' the woman offered hesitantly.

'No, that's not necessary.' Sabrina wanted solitude and quiet to get her chaotic senses back in order.

'I'll wait out here for you then.'

'No,' Sabrina refused swiftly, then drew a breath and made her voice sound calm. 'I can make it back on my own. I can't keep you from your guests. Just give me an idea of where I am and I'll find my way back. I'm really quite good at following directions.'

The older woman hesitated, then gave Sabrina a simple set of directions to follow back to the main party area. After thanking her, and assuring her again that she was all right, Sabrina walked unerringly to the door, aware that her hostess watched. Fortunately no one else was in the room and Sabrina had it to herself. The closed door reduced the voices to a low hum.

The exploring tip of her cane touched a chair leg. Sighing heavily, Sabrina sank on to the velvet cushion. A vanity table was in front of her and she rested her arms on its smooth top. But the silence didn't stop the racing of her mind.

She had always wondered — she had always questioned Bay's motive for seeing her. Secretly she had stopped believing it was because of pity. Bay had used the word compassion, but not even that less offensive word eased the stabbing hurt of the conversation she had overheard. And he was letting pity for her serve a twofold purpose. While he was charitably spending a night or two a week with Sabrina, he was trying to make this Roni jealous.

Her fingers balled into tight fists. Damn this acute hearing! She moaned silently. No, another voice inside remonstrated her, she should be glad she had discovered his real motive. She was lucky she had regarded him as nothing more than a friend and had found out the truth before she had begun to misinterpret his attention. How awful it would have been if she had started to care for him as a man!

The problem was — what was the next step? Should she confront him with what she had learned? That was what she wanted to do. She wanted to throw his charitable, pitying words in his face. But what good would that do? He would simply deny it as he had all the other times.

Bay Cameron was smooth and cannily intelligent — that was something Sabrina mustn't overlook. Look at the way he had maneuvered her first into accepting the ivory cane she used, then going out to dinner at a public restaurant and finally coming here tonight to this party of strangers. Well, the last had backfired. Now Sabrina knew his true colors.

The door opened and a woman walked in. Her voice as she greeted Sabrina was familiar, but she couldn't recall the woman's name. Self-consciously Sabrina smoothed the back of her hair, pretending that she was in front of the vanity table checking her appearance. With fingers crossed, she hoped the woman wouldn't tarry long. Unfortunately she did, and each passing second ticked loudly in Sabrina's head.

At last Sabrina knew she couldn't stay any longer without arousing suspicion. She had already been in the room a considerable time. She didn't want Mrs. Thyssen sending a search party for her. If only she could slip away from the house, she wished, as she rose to her feet. She didn't want to go back to the party. It was taking on the overtones of a nightmare.

But where would she go, she asked herself, pushing open the door to the hall. Even if she could sneak away unseen, there was little likelihood there would be a taxi cab cruising in this residential neighborhood. She doubted very much if she could hold her tongue during the long ride home with Bay.

Not concentrating on where she was going, she bumped into a small table sitting against the wall of the hallway. Instinctively her hand reached out to prevent whatever was on the table from falling to the floor. A vase had started to tip, but she set it upright again. As she started to withdraw her hand, her fingers encountered a familiarly smooth object — the receiver of a telephone.

There was the answer! Not caring who might be observing her action, Sabrina picked up the receiver, her fingers quickly dialing Information and requesting the number of a taxi company. Without allowing any time for second thoughts, she dialed the number given her.

When the phone was answered on the other end, Sabrina said quietly, 'Would you please send a cab to —' She stopped. She didn't know where she was. Footsteps were approaching. 'Just a moment,' she requested the man on the other end of the line to wait. Taking a deep breath, she turned to the person coming nearer. She had to take a chance. 'Excuse me, please, but would you tell me what the address is here?'

'Yes, ma'am,' a courteous female voice replied, and gave her the address.

The studied politeness of the woman's voice prompted Sabrina to ask, 'Are — are you the maid?'

'Yes, ma'am,' the woman answered in a voice that said she had noticed the white cane in Sabrina's hand.

'Would you bring me my jacket? It's a black rabbit fur,' Sabrina requested.

'Right away, ma'am.'

At the departing footsteps, Sabrina removed her hand from the mouthpiece and gave the address to the man patiently waiting on the other end. He promised only a few minutes' wait. With the receiver safely in its cradle, Sabrina turned away from the table. The smell of success was intoxicatingly near.

Footsteps approached again from the direction the maid had taken. Sabrina could not tell if it was the maid and she held her breath, fearful that at any second she would be discovered by Bay or Mrs. Thyssen.

'Here you are, ma'am,' the maid spoke. 'Shall I help you on with it?'

'Please,' Sabrina agreed nervously.

The maid deftly helped her into the fur jacket. 'Shall I let Mrs. Thyssen know you're leaving?'

'No, that won't be necessary. I've already spoken to her,' she lied hurriedly. 'The cab will be here any minute. I'll wait outside. The front door, is it straight ahead down this hall?'

'Yes, ma'am,' the maid acknowledged. 'But the fog is rather thick tonight. It would be best to wait inside.'

'I'd prefer the fresh air. The smoke has got a bit thick in here.' She didn't want to risk being discovered when she was so near her goal.

'Very well, ma'am,' the maid submitted, and silently withdrew.

As quickly as her searching cane would permit, Sabrina traveled the length of the hallway to the front door. Her palms were perspiring with excitement as she opened the front door and stepped into the night.

The cool air was a soothing balm to her taut nerve ends. She moved away from the door, seeking the shadows she knew would be at the side of the entrance. The damp fog was heavy against her face. The thick walls of the house shut out the noise within. The sleeping night was profoundly still.

A smile turned up the corners of her wide mouth as she imagined Bay's confusion when he discovered she was gone. His overworked sense of pity would have him concerned for her safety, but she knew it wouldn't be long before the maid would be questioned. She would tell him that Sabrina had taken a taxi. He would be angry, but at this point Sabrina didn't care. Whatever debt she might have thought she owed him for his assistance and supposed friendship had been paid in full tonight.

Time went by slowly, but it always seemed to double its length when she was waiting anxiously for something. Sabrina remained in the shadows, hopefully concealed from anyone who might decide to leave the party early. Finally the steady growl of a car motor sounded down the street. She waited to see if it stopped at this house or continued past. It halted at the curb and a car door slammed.

As she stepped from the shadows, a man's voice asked curtly, 'Did you call for a cab, lady?'

'Yes, I did.' She walked as swiftly as she could toward him, victory lightening her step. A car door opened. She used the sound to judge the distance. The man's hand took her elbow to help her into the rear of the cab. 'I want you to take me to —'

Sabrina never got the address of her home out. The front door of the house opened and the hairs on the back of her neck stood out, freezing her muscles into immobility. She had nearly made it.

Maybe she still could. There wasn't much time. Bay's long strides were already eating up the distance from the front door to the taxi.

As she tried to slip into the rear seat, an arm circled her waist, a hand spreading across the flat of her stomach and drawing her back to the sidewalk.

'Let me go!' She struggled against the steel band that held her mercilessly.

'Be still, Sabrina,' Bay ordered, only tightening his hold. There was the crisp sound of money being removed from his pocket. 'I'm sorry you were called out unnecessarily,' he was talking to the cab driver. 'I'll see her home.'

86

'I don't want to go with you,' she protested vigorously. The driver had not moved, and there was a chance he could be an ally. 'Please, tell this man to leave me alone.'

'Will you stop involving others in our quarrels?' Bay demanded curtly. The implication of his demand was that they were having a little spat, a ruse on Bay's part to assure the driver that his assistance was not really needed.

There was a crisp exchange of money before the man wished Bay good luck and Sabrina knew her means of escape was lost. For a deflated moment she stopped struggling to free herself from Bay's pinning grip while the cab driver closed the rear door and walked around to the other side.

Turning her at right angles, his hand shifted to the side of her waist as he forced her to walk away from the departing taxi. Bay did not lead her back to the house but toward his car parked at the curb some distance down the street.

'Would you like to explain to me what's going on?' he requested grimly in a voice that was not at all amused.

'Surely it's obvious. I was going home,' Sabrina retorted.

'If you wanted to leave, why didn't you look for me? I never said we had to stay at the party until the last minute.' His fingers were biting into the soft flesh of her waist.

'I didn't want *you* to take me home, that's why!' she snapped.

'Then you should have left your cane behind. Maybe no one would have noticed you leaving if it hadn't been for that little white stick!' He was angry. It vibrated through his tautly controlled voice.

'If I'd given it a thought, I would have.' She refused to be intimidated by his tightly held temper.

'And why, after all this time, would you suddenly not want me to take you home?' Bay demanded.

'I don't need a reason,' Sabrina answered haughtily.

'Yes, you do, and before this night is out, I'm going to hear it,' he informed her with unrelenting arrogance.

Sabrina stopped short and Bay did likewise. 'Maybe I'm tired of your pity and your patronizing attitude!' she challenged boldly, tilting her head so he could see the dislike in her expression. 'I don't need you or anybody else to feel sorry for me!'

'What?' She could sense his frowning alertness.

'Go and join the Boy Scouts!' Her voice grew shrill. 'I'm tired of your good deeds!' There was a traitorous quiver of her chin.

'Pity! Is that what you think I feel?' The accusation exploded around her.

Sabrina opened her mouth to retaliate, and in the next instant she was jerked against him. The violence of his action sent her cane clattering on to the sidewalk. An arm curved punishingly between her shoulder blades. His hand gripped the back of her neck, forcing her head back while he drew her on to tiptoes.

Her startled cry was smothered by his hard mouth. Roughly, almost savagely he kissed her, not allowing her to draw a breath as he ground her lips against her teeth.

An elemental tension crackled in the air when he raised his head. His hands moved, closing over the slender bones of her shoulders, keeping Sabrina in front of him.

'You're a brute and a bully, Bay Cameron!' The hissing accusation was offered between gasps for air.

'Then I might as well be hanged for a sinner as a saint!' The harsh words carried the steel edge of sarcasm.

Again he gathered her to his chest, pinning her against the rock wall while the muscles in his arms rippled around her. Sabrina had not recovered from the brutal pressure of his first kiss when she was punished by the second. She strained against him weakly, her strength ebbing from the riptide of his embrace.

As her resistance faded, an angry passion was transmitted to her by his demanding lips. A feverish warmth enveloped her and unwillingly her flesh began to respond to the hard commanding mouth that possessed hers.

Mindlessly her hands stopped pushing against him and her fingers curled into the lapels of his jacket. Through the rainbow explosion of her senses, Sabrina realized she was falling victim to the very virility she had warned herself against.

As suddenly as it all began, it ended with Bay firmly holding her an arm's length away. Her equilibrium was completely gone. Up was down and down was up. It was a topsy-turvy world, this midnight velvet blackness she lived in. And it was because of Bay and his punishing embrace.

'Get in the car!' The harsh command was like a physical slap in the face.

But even the abrupt jolt to reality couldn't prod Sabrina into movement. Finally Bay dragged, carried, and shoved her into the passenger seat. Her voice didn't return until he was behind the wheel and driving the car away from the curb.

'Bay —' Her weak voice was barely above a whisper.

'Shut up, Sabrina.' The terse, grating tone of his voice indicated that the words were drawn through clenched jaws. 'Maybe when I can think clearly, I'll be able to offer an apology. Right now all I want to do is wring your bloody neck!'

Eight

Obeying his command, Sabrina had not spoken during that tense ride to her home. She had been too frightened to speak — not because she had thought he would carry out his threat or that he would subject her again to the punishment of his kisses. Sabrina had been frightened by herself. For a few fleeting moments in his arms, she had not been a blind woman, only a woman.

Her bruised mouth had retained the burning fire of his hard, demanding kiss. The racing of her heart had kept pounding in her ears as if she was on a runaway locomotive that she couldn't jump off. The impression of those muscled arms that had locked her in his embrace had still been felt.

Her breast and hips had remembered the solid rock pressure of his chest and thighs, implanting the hard male outline of his body so firmly in her mind that Sabrina thought she would never be able to uproot it. The scent of his maleness and spicy cologne had clung to her skin. Nothing had seemed to remove it.

What was worse, she didn't want to erase anything. That was why she was still frightened two days after the fact. Over and over again she had asked herself why he had kissed her that way.

Had the brutally volatile embrace been prompted by anger that she had found out his true motive? Could he have used her as an outlet for frustration because his plan to make the girl Roni jealous had failed? In view of the conversation she had overheard, it was the most likely explanation. Probably it was a combination of several things.

Sabrina would not consider the possibility that Bay had been prompted by any physical desire for her. Not that she believed that there would not be a time when she would meet some man who truly loved and wanted her. But visualizing Bay Cameron as that man was something she could not do. He had position, wealth, charm, and looks. There were too many other women he could have at his side in an intimate sense.

Her blindness had touched him. It didn't matter which noun was used to identify the emotion he felt — pity, compassion, sympathy. They were all one and the same thing.

Pain gnawed at her heart. Pride said that she couldn't regard Bay as a friend any longer. A true friend might commiserate, but he would never seek her company because he felt sorry for her. But Sabrina's heart honestly acknowledged the main reason why she must reject him. She was the one who had stopped regarding him as a friend and had started thinking of him as a man. For her, that was dangerously foolish.

A sob rasped her throat, choking her with its futility. Sabrina buried her face in her hands, letting the misery wash over her. For a little time in the solitude of this afternoon, she would feel sorry for herself and not regret it. She had earned the right.

Before the first tears slipped from her brown eyes, the telephone rang. 'No!' Sabrina denied its call softly. But it persisted.

The urge was there to ignore it, to let it ring until the person on the other end gave up. Grimacing at the possibility that it was her father, she knew she had no right to cause him unnecessary concern. Reluctantly she rose to her feet and walked to the telephone.

'Lane residence,' she answered in a pseudo-calm voice.

'Sabrina.'

The sound of Bay's low husky voice nearly made her drop the telephone. It was as if a bolt of lightning had struck her. A weakness quaked her knees and she quickly sought the support of a chair.

'Are you there, Sabrina?' his frowning voice asked when she failed to reply immediately.

'Yes, hello, Bay.' Her reply was strained and unnatural, but it didn't matter any more.

'How are you?' It was not a casual question. There was too much guarded alertness in his tone.

'Fine. And you?' She was purposely distant and polite.

Bay ignored her aloof inquiry. 'You know why I've called, don't you?'

'How could I possibly know that?' Sabrina asked with cutting disinterest.

'Would you have dinner with me Saturday night?' A grimness changed the invitation into a challenge.

But Sabrina had guessed that if Bay did make any conciliatory gesture as he had indicated he might, it would be wrapped in a suggestion for a Saturday night date. She realized now that he always chose Saturday night because that was the evening her father devoted exclusively to Deborah and Sabrina spent it alone — at least, she had for the most part before she met Bay. Yesterday she had invited an old friend, Sally Goodwin, over on Saturday night.

'I've already made other plans,' she answered truthfully and a shade triumphantly.

'You have?' The mocking inflection doubted her statement.

'I do know other people besides you, Bay,' she retorted.

A tired yet angry sigh came over the wire. 'May I take a guess that you *arranged* to be busy on Saturday night?'

'You may guess if you want,' she shrugged, neither affirming or denying.

'May I also guess that because of my — indiscretion the other night, you've decided not to see me again?' He didn't let her reply. 'You didn't make any allowances for the possibility that I might have had the right to lose my temper because you walked out without even having the courtesy to leave a message that you were leaving? I probably should have turned you over my knee, but the other seemed more appropriate at the time.'

There was some validity to his argument, but Sabrina was not going to allow herself to be swayed. 'It's done. There isn't any point in discussing it.'

'Then that's your decision. You aren't going to see me again,' Bay stated with almost arrogant blandness. 'Those few moments of my anger wiped out all the memories of the hours, enjoyable hours I thought, that we spent together before. Is that right? They mean nothing to you?'

His challenge had to be answered. 'Yes, they did,' Sabrina admitted coldly, 'until they were tarnished by the discovery that you felt sorry for me. I told you once I don't need anyone's pity.'

'Who in their right mind would feel sorry for a pigheaded, spoiled brat like you?' he snapped. He drew a deep, calming breath. 'There are times, Sabrina, when you test a man's patience. How many times do I have to tell you that I don't feel sorry for you before you'll believe me?'

'Then explain to me why you see me,' she demanded defiantly.

'There has to be an ulterior motive, is that it?' Bay answered grimly. 'It can't be because I might —' he paused an instant, choosing his words '— admire you, your courage when you aren't being unreasonably stubborn. Let me put the question to you. Why do you go out with me? Am I a convenient means to get out of the house? Do you simply tolerate me because I take you places you want to go? What's your ulterior motive, Sabrina?'

'I . . . I have none,' she answered, taken aback by his counterattack.

'Come now. Surely you must,' he mocked derisively. 'You had to have a reason for going out with me.'

'No, I don't,' Sabrina insisted in helpless confusion, 'I simply enjoyed it. I had —'

Bay interrupted. 'Yet it's inconceivable that I might have simply enjoyed your company, too?'

'How could you?' she protested, seeking to regain the offensive. 'I'm pigheaded and spoiled. You said so yourself.'

'So? I'm arrogant and a bully. You said so yourself.' He deflected her argument with mocking humor. 'That makes us equal with two flaws apiece.'

The corners of her mouth twitched in reluctant amusement. Her stand against him was weakening. She could feel the firm resolve crumbling under his persuasive charm and logic.

'You're smiling, aren't you, Sabrina?' he accused softly. 'Don't bother to answer,' Bay chuckled. 'I know you'll deny it. I won't ask you to cancel your well-laid plans for Saturday night, but come sailing with me Sunday.'

'Sailing?' she echoed weakly. Of all the invitations Bay could have extended, her own love of the sport made this one she wanted least to refuse.

'Yes, sailing,' he repeated with amused patience.

'I —' Sabrina couldn't get the words of refusal to come out.

'I'll pick you up bright and early Sunday morning around seven. We'll spend the day.'

'I . . . I'll be ready.' Her words of acceptance stumbled over each other in their rush to get out before better judgment decreed that she change her mind.

'At seven a.m. Sunday,' Bay agreed, and hung up as if he had the same thought.

Sabrina didn't change her mind. She had a multitude of second thoughts, but none of them had lasted long enough to bring her to the point of canceling. Any thought that her father might take the decision out of her hands had ended the same day Bay had called.

When she had told her father of Bay's invitation that evening, his reply had been: 'Yes, Bay called me this afternoon to be certain I had no objections. I don't, and I promise you I won't worry. You'll be in good hands. Besides, Bay can swim.'

Sunday morning, therefore, found Sabrina aboard his trim ketch *Dame Fortune*. Fog and dormant wind had delayed their departure for nearly an hour.

Now they were under sail, the stiff breeze ruffling the scarf tied around Sabrina's head, the salty taste of ocean spray on her lips. Passing under the rust-orange span of the Golden Gate Bridge, Bay had turned southward into the open sea, past Cliff House and Seal Rocks. He continued beyond the ocean beaches, the treacherous undertow in the area restricting their use to sunbathing and walking.

As always, Sabrina champed at the constricting life-vest tied around her even while she accepted the wisdom of the precaution whether for sighted or unsighted boaters. The deck was slanted sharply beneath her, heaving with each ocean swell, as Bay expertly took advantage of all the wind he could and still remain on course.

The billowing wind in the canvas, the ocean waves slapping the sleek hull, and the comfortable groans of a sailing ketch at sea were the only sounds around her. She had hardly exchanged five words with Bay since they had left the Yacht Harbor. Conversation wasn't necessary and would have been superfluous to the serene beauty of the moment. Each seemed to sense the other's deep pleasure and nothing needed to be said.

It was some time before Sabrina noticed there had been a change in their course. The sun was not in the place it normally would have been in their initial heading. Blocking out the song of sea and sail, she listened intently, trying to gauge by memory and sound their location and failing.

She turned to Bay. 'Where are we?'

'In the waters of Monterey Bay near Santa Cruz. Were you daydreaming?' he smiled with his voice.

Instantly she visualized his ruggedly forceful features, tanned by the sun and the wind, cinnamon brown hair dampened by the salt spray and tousled by the breeze. The sun was directly overhead. His light brown eyes would be narrowed against its brilliance, crinkled at the corners because of that flashing smile she had detected in his voice. It was disturbing how vividly clear her picture of him was, so vitally alive and masculine.

Her heart beat a rapid tattoo against her ribs. 'Daydreaming or seadreaming. I don't know which,' she murmured.

Again there was a change in the motion of the ketch. The wind was catching less canvas and their speed had decreased. The deck beneath her had begun to right itself.

'What are you doing now?' Sabrina asked.

'Taking her in close to shore. We just passed the natural bridges north of Santa Cruz. I thought we'd anchor south of Santa Cruz for lunch. There's a small quiet cove I know about that I hope no one else has discovered.'

Once anchored, with Sabrina giving what assistance she could, the only sound was the gentle lapping of the almost calm surf against the hull. She turned her head inquiringly toward Bay and felt his gaze moving over her face. A fiery warmth started in her midsection. She was suddenly and intensely aware that they were alone, the two of them, a man and a woman. She put brakes to that thought sharply.

'I'll go below and fix lunch.' She pivoted abruptly away. 'What are we having?'

'Sandwiches, salad and the like. It's all fixed,' Bay answered. 'What about a swim before we eat? The water is warmer here than up the coast and there aren't any dangerous undercurrents.'

'Sorry,' Sabrina shrugged away his suggestion nervously. 'You didn't warn me to bring a swimming suit and I didn't.'

'That doesn't matter.' Bay dismissed her excuse. 'I always keep a few swimming clothes on board in case there's a spur-of-the-moment decision by one of my guests to take a dip in the ocean. I'm sure one of them will fit you.'

'But —' She hadn't been in any water other than her bathtub since before the accident.

'But what?' he prompted. 'You can swim, can't you?'

'Yes, I can swim,' she swallowed tightly.

'I'll point you in the right direction so you won't head out to sea if you're worrying about losing your reference points. Go and change.'

He told her in which locker he kept the spare swimming suits and Sabrina went below. It was better to go swimming with the wide limits of the ocean and shore than remaining on the small deck alone with him.

Most of the swimsuits were two-piece outfits, some bare triangles of cloth. Sabrina chose the close-fitting knit of a one-piece with diamond cut-outs at the waist crisscrossed with ties. At least in it she felt less naked when she walked up on deck. Her long hair was let down and curling around her shoulders. The water would have pulled it free of its knot eventually, so she had done it first.

'I'm ready,' she said nervously.

Bay didn't comment on her appearance. 'I've put a rope ladder over the side.' He took her hand and led her to the rail. 'I'll go in the water first.'

When he released her hand after her silent nod of agreement, Sabrina tightened the hand into a fist to retain the warmth of his touch a while longer. It was a stupid thing to do. This was not a romantic outing but a friendly one — which was why the sensations she was feeling were troubling her.

The deck rocked slightly, followed by the sound of something slicing into the water, and Sabrina knew that Bay had not used the ladder but had dived into the water. A second later she heard him surface, turning her head in the direction of the sound. A few clean strokes brought him to the bottom of the ladder.

'Come on in. The water's fine,' he called to her.

While Bay held the ladder steady, Sabrina started down, her toes feeling for the rope rungs. In the water which was neither warm nor cold, Sabrina clung to the security of the ladder for a few minutes, adjusting to the eerie sensation of having nothing solid beneath her feet. The chattering of her teeth was from nerves and not the tepidly cool water.

'Are you ready?' Bay was still beside the ladder.

'I think so,' Sabrina answered, clenching her jaw so he wouldn't hear the clatter of her teeth.

He moved a few strokes from the ladder, then said, 'Swim toward my voice.'

Forcing her hand to release its death-grip on the rope, Sabrina took a deep breath and struck out toward him. At first she was hampered by nervousness and uncoordination, but they soon faded as she became accustomed to the watery environment. She could hear Bay's firm cleaving strokes keeping pace beside her and drew strength and assurance from his presence.

It seemed as if they had been swimming a long time. Sabrina had begun to get tired. Her reaching arms were beginning to feel heavy. She stopped to tread water and catch her breath, and Bay did the same.

'How much farther?' she asked as she swallowed down gulps of air.

'About another fifteen feet before we can touch bottom.' He sounded not at all out of breath. 'Can you make it?'

She didn't answer but started out again, maintaining a slow steady rhythm that would not wear her out too quickly. Surprisingly it didn't seem as if she had traveled any distance at all before a kicking foot scraped the sandy bottom. Sabrina righted herself quickly, wiping the salt water from her face and tucking her long wet hair behind her ears.

'You made it,' Bay spoke from somewhere near her left side. 'How do you feel?'

She smiled faintly. 'Exhausted, but good otherwise.'

'Let's go ashore and take a breather.'

Her hands were lightly resting on top of the almost chest-high water, letting the gentle swells roll over them. The waves would have told her which way the shore was if she had been in doubt, but Bay took her hand anyway and led her to the beach.

'This beach comes equipped with its own sunning rock,' he said as they waded on to the sandy ground, smooth and firm beneath her feet. 'It's a little hard, but it's better than the sand when you don't have a towel.' The pressure of his hand stopped her after they had gone a few yards. 'Here.'

Before Sabrina could protest, his hands were around her waist and he was lifting her on to the hard, warm surface of the stone. Her own fingers had automatically gripped the sinewy wetness of his arms for balance. Her flesh burned where his hands had covered the open diamond patches of the swimsuit waistline. It was several seconds before her racing heart settled to a more respectable pace. By then he was on the rock, too.

'Did you have a good time last night?' he asked after he had moved into a comfortable position. He was sitting. Sabrina could tell by the direction of his voice.

'Last night?' she frowned, and shifted more fully on to the rock. Then she remembered. 'Yes, I did.' Actually it had been a quiet evening. She and Sally had sat around and talked, listening to records part of the time.

'Where did you go?'

'Nowhere, Sally and I stayed at the house,' she shrugged, turning her face to the warmth of the sun, letting it chase away the shivers on her damp skin.

'An evening of gossipy girl-talk, is that it?' There was a mocking smile in his tone.

Sabrina wasn't certain whether he was laughing at her uneventful evening or that she had chosen it over one with him. From what she knew of Bay, the first seemed more likely.

'Men gossip as much as if not more than women,' she replied.

He didn't argue the point. 'I suppose it's true of an equal number in each sex.'

An awkward silence followed. At least it was awkward for Sabrina. She was too aware of Bay, physically aware of him. She leaned back on her hands.

'The sun feels good,' she suggested.

'I think I'll stretch out and enjoy it,' Bay stated.

At the same time that he spoke, his movements were carrying out his words. And the silence that Sabrina had not wanted reigned, broken only by the slow rush of the ocean on to shore. There was little for her to do except to follow suit.

Her searching hands found a small, elevated hump in the rock behind her, a natural headrest, and Sabrina lay down on her back. For a long time she listened to the sound of Bay's even breathing. Her own was shallow, her chest muscles constricted with tension. Finally the heat of the sun and the rock coaxed her into relaxing.

Sabrina didn't fall asleep, but she did drift into that strange state of half-sleep. She was aware of her surroundings and the man beside her, yet deaf to them at the same time. Then something brought all of her senses alert. Her eyes blinked uselessly as she tried to determine what had disturbed her. She turned her head slightly in Bay's direction and accidentally brushed his hand with her cheek. Then her sensitive nerve ends transmitted the message that he was holding a lock of her silky brown hair.

'Do you know this is the first time I've ever seen you wear your hair down?' he mused softly.

'I — I don't like to wear it down. It gets in the way.' There was an odd tremor in her voice as she guessed how close he was to her. She could almost feel the heat of his body stretched beside hers. His voice had come from a position slightly above her, indicating that he was possibly lying on his side, an elbow propping him up.

Bay didn't seem to pay any attention to her explanation.

'When you wear your hair up in that little topknot, you look poised and sophisticated, a well-bred young queen. With your hair down like this,' he twined the strand around his finger, 'there's a gamin vulnerability about you.'

A pulse was beating wildly in her temples. It was impossible to roll away from him. The edge of the rock was too near.

'Do you think we should be heading back?' Her throat was taut, making her voice likewise.

'What's the matter?' he mocked. 'Don't you like my comments on your hairstyle?'

'It doesn't matter.' Sabrina shook her head determinedly, loosing the lock of hair against her bare shoulder. 'I'm going to wear it up because it's the easiest to take care of, regardless of how you prefer it.' It was a challenging statement, but she didn't care.

Bay reached back and gave her hair a sharp tug. 'Then you'll probably be sorry to hear that I prefer that silky knot. The way it is now would be appropriate for the privacy of a bedroom.'

The sensual implication of his statement drew a sharp breath from Sabrina. Her heightened awareness of his masculinity made this type of conversation impossible. She wasn't capable of idle flirtation, this suggestive playing with words. She started to push herself back into a half-sitting position to escape his nearness, but Bay was already straightening to his feet.

'We'll head back,' he said as he towered above her.

Sabrina thankfully swung her legs to the edge of the rock. Bay was on the sand, his hands gripping her waist to lift her down before she could slide the short distance to the sand. Straining away from his unwanted assistance, her effort to keep from landing too close to him brought a heel down on a partially buried outcropping of the rock. The unexpected jarring pain sent her against his chest. His hold tightened to steady her.

'Are you all right?'

Her unspoken answer was negative. It couldn't be otherwise when the nakedness of his muscled torso and thighs pressed against her was playing havoc with her heart. Soft, curling chest hairs sensually tickled her palms. His head was inclined toward her, warm breath stirring a wing of her dark bangs.

The desire was strong to slide her arms around his broad shoulders and nestle her head against his neck. To resist the nearly overpowering impulse, she moistened her lips nervously and tipped her head back.

'I'm all right,' she assured him in a shaking voice. 'I stepped on a rock or something.'

A sudden breath of wind tossed a thin lock of hair across her face. It clung to the gleaming wetness of her lips. Sabrina started to push it away, but her hand was only part way there when Bay's fingers drew it gently away, pushing it back with the rest of her long hair.

His hand remained along the side of her face, his thumb absently caressing her cheekbone. She held her breath, motion suspended under the magical spell of his touch.

The heady warmth of his firm mouth was barely felt against hers before Sabrina sharply twisted her head away. Her defences couldn't endure a casual kiss.

'Don't, Bay, please!' she requested stiffly.

'I wasn't going to hurt you.' Her words brought a rigid stillness to his touch as he misinterpreted the reason for the shudders quivering through her.

'I simply don't want you to kiss me,' Sabrina stated, pulling free of his unresisting arms and taking several quick steps away until common sense warned her that she couldn't see where she was going.

She wrapped her arms tightly around her, trying to fight off the chill that shivered over her where the warmth of his body had been.

Bay walked over to stand beside her. She could feel his eyes boring into her. Her lashes fluttered downward in case her sightless eyes mirrored the heady sensations swimming in her mind. For an electric moment, she hardly dared to breathe.

'We'd better head back to the boat.' The savage bite of his words betrayed a tightly leashed anger. Sabrina couldn't tell if it was directed at himself or at her.

The hand that gripped hers and led her toward the water was cold and impersonal. Sabrina was glad when the water became deep enough to swim and he had to release her. She hadn't thought it possible that his touch, which usually started a fire, could chill her to the bone.

It was not a leisurely swim back. Sabrina set herself a pace that took every ounce of her strength to maintain. It was a form of self-punishment for being so foolish as to let Bay persuade her to come to this outing when wisdom had dictated that she stop seeing him.

She was completely spent when Bay reached out and pulled her to the rope ladder, but she climbed aboard without his assistance. She paused on deck to catch her breath.

'If we'd been anchored another ten feet away, you would never have made it. What were you trying to prove?' Bay snapped.

'Nothing.' Sabrina averted her head and self-consciously felt her way to the steps leading below deck.

'When you're dressed, you can get the lunch ready. I think you can find everything. In the meantime, I'll get us under way,' he ordered tersely.

'Don't you . . . Don't you want to eat first?' she faltered.

'I think we're both in a hurry to get back, aren't we?' There was a derisive challenge in his voice that dared her to deny it. When she didn't reply, he added grimly, 'I'll enjoy the food as much as you once we're under sail.'

Actually Sabrina found the food tasteless. Most of it wanted to stick in her throat, but she forced as much of it down as she could. There was no atmosphere of friendliness on the return trip. Their mutual silence was brittle with tension.

Bay's acceptance of her polite words of thanks at the conclusion of the day was as cool and aloof as her offer had been. When the iron gate closed behind him, Sabrina knew why she was so totally miserable. She had plenty of time to ponder the reason on the way back. She had fallen in love with Bay Cameron. She was literally a blind fool.

Nine

Bay's last parting remark to her had been 'I'll call you.' In Sabrina's experience, those particular words had always signaled the end of a relationship. It was Friday night and he had not phoned.

Another tear slipped down her cheek. She wiped it away with her fingertips, leaving a streak of dark clay to smudge her face. Why couldn't her tear ducts have been damaged as well as her eyesight? she wondered forlornly, then sighed. Perhaps it was better to have a way to release the pain.

There was a knock on the studio door. She had kept it closed this last week, not wanting anyone to pop in without at least the warning click of the doorknob. She had told her father it was because she wanted to block out any distractions. The truth was she could work in the middle of rush hour traffic. Lately, however, she had discovered herself simply standing and crying. It was this she didn't want her father or anyone else to see.

Sabrina took the hem of her smock and wiped her face carefully just in case there was a betraying tear she had missed. 'Come in,' she called in answer to the knock.

A cloud of perfume swirled into the room, a scent her mind labeled as Deborah's. The lightly graceful steps confirmed the identification.

'I came to remind you we would be leaving in an hour so you would have plenty of time to clean up here and change clothes,' her future stepmother said brightly.

'I don't think I'll go,' Sabrina murmured, centering her attention on the partially completed clay bust on the work pedestal.

'Grant has been looking forward to the three of us dining out tonight,' Deborah reminded her.

'I know, but I'd rather keep working a while longer. I'm right in the middle of this piece. I want to keep going while the concept is still fresh in my mind,' she lied.

'Are you sure?' came the slightly troubled question.

'I've just really grasped the form, and I don't want to lose it,' Sabrina assured her.

'I didn't mean about the work,' Deborah said hesitantly.

'What did you mean, then?' Her hand was poised along the half-formed ear of the bust. Was Deborah's womanly intuition at work?

'I . . . I wanted to be sure you weren't refusing because of me. I don't want you to think you would be the superfluous third tonight,' the attractive redhead explained self-consciously.

'No, Deborah, it wasn't because of you.' Sabrina expelled a silent sigh of relief. 'We'll go out another night. I probably shouldn't have started this so late, but now that I have, I must work a little longer.'

'I understand. I know how important this is to you. And don't worry, Sabrina.' There was the warmth of a smile in her voice. 'I'll explain to Grant.'

'What were you going to explain to me?'

'Grant!' Deborah exclaimed in a startled voice. 'You shouldn't sneak up on a person like that.'

'I didn't sneak. You simply didn't hear me.' There was the faint sound of a kiss exchanged. 'Now, I repeat, what are you going to explain to me?'

Sabrina answered for Deborah. 'I've decided to stay and work tonight instead of going out to dinner with you two.'

'The two of us were going out to dinner with you, not the other way round,' her father frowned.

'Then we'll go out another night,' she shrugged, determined not to let him change her mind.

'No, we'll go out tonight.'

'Grant!' Deborah interjected a silent plea into his name.

'Dammit, she's working too hard, Deborah,' he declared forcefully. 'Look at the dark circles under her eyes and the hollows in her cheeks. She doesn't sleep. She doesn't eat. All she does is work from dawn to dusk, or more aptly midnight.'

'Dad, you're exaggerating,' Sabrina sighed. 'Besides, my work is important to me.' It was the only thing that kept her sanity. Without it, the emptiness of a life without Bay would be more than she could stand. 'I promise as soon as I can leave this piece I'm doing I'll fix myself something to eat and go straight to bed. How's that?'

'I think that's a fair bargain, don't you, Grant?' Deborah murmured.

'I—' He took a deep, angry breath, but arguing with the two women he loved was not something he enjoyed. He sighed heavily. 'All right,' he surrendered. 'You can stay home this time. But next week we're all going out together, with no excuses. Now, why don't you let me have a peep at this work of art that is too important to leave?'

Sabrina stepped to the side as he walked closer. 'I only have it roughed in right now. I'm doing the head and shoulders of Gino Marchetti as he was in his youth. Over a year ago, he showed me a picture taken at his wedding. I had intended to do a painting, but —' She left that unfinished for obvious reasons. 'He looked very Roman, very proud and very strong.'

'Gino, the druggist?' Grant Lane repeated with a hint of disbelief.

'It's only rough,' Sabrina defended.

There was a moment of silence as he studied the partially completed head of the bust. Then he turned suddenly. 'Deborah, who does it look like to you?'

'Well —' Her hesitation was pronounced. 'I don't know Gino very well.'

'I've known him for years. I'm sorry to be the one to tell you, Sabrina, but that doesn't look like him at all, not even when he was younger,' he said emphatically.

'When it's finished —' Sabrina began.

'It will look exactly like Bay Cameron,' her father finished the sentence for her.

'You must be mistaken,' she responded evenly, but she clenched her hands tightly together until they hurt, punishing them for having betrayed her. 'It doesn't look at all like Bay, does it, Deborah?'

'It does bear a slight resemblance to him,' the other woman admitted reluctantly, 'but as you said, it isn't finished.'

'The man has an interesting face. If you could see it, Sabrina, I know you would have had the urge to put it on canvas. But nevertheless, I'm not going to argue with you. You're the artist not me. If you say it's Gino, it's Gino. I suppose there's Roman characteristics in both of them.' He put his arm around her shoulders and gave her a reassuring hug. 'Now if you two ladies will excuse me, I came up here to shower and change.'

After bestowing a light kiss on Sabrina's cheek, he left the room. Sabrina stared sightlessly at the mound of clay on the work pedestal, her heart crying with pain. For a moment she had forgotten Deborah was still in the room, until the faint click of a heel reminded her.

'Sabrina, about Bay —' The gentle voice paused.

'What about Bay?' Sabrina challenged, her tone cold and aloof.

'You aren't becoming . . . too involved with him, are you?' Deborah faltered as if sensing she was trespassing on private territory. 'I mean, I admire him very much, but I don't think you should —'

'— take his attentions too seriously,' Sabrina finished for her. 'I'm well aware that he only sees me to be kind.' She couldn't bring herself to use the word pity.

'I'm glad.' There was a faint sigh of relief in the redhead's statement. 'I'm sure he likes you, Sabrina. I just don't think it would be wise if you became too fond of him. After all you've been through, it wouldn't be fair.'

'I am fond of him,' she asserted. 'He helped me a great deal. Bay was even the one to suggest that I try working in clay.' Silently she admitted that it wasn't a fair trade to give away her heart for a career, but when was anything connected with love classified as fair? 'But don't worry, Deborah. I haven't misinterpreted his motives.'

'You always seem to have your feet on the ground,' was the faintly envious response.

Only this time my head was in the clouds, Sabrina thought to herself. She mumbled an absent reply when Deborah said she would leave Sabrina to her work.

As the studio door closed behind her father's red-haired fiancée, Sabrina's hands reached tentatively toward the bust, lightly exploring the roughed-in features, confirming for herself that indeed it was Bay. A cold anger pervaded her body.

Destroy it! Smash it! her mind ordered. Turn it back into an ordinary lump of clay!

Her hands rested on either side of the face, but they couldn't carry out the order. One tear fell, then another. Finally silent sobs racked her slender form, her shoulders hunching forward at the excruciating pain in her chest.

But her hands didn't remain immobile. Shakily they began working, painstakingly defining each detail of his face in the molding clay. It was a labor of love, and what pieces of her heart she hadn't given to Bay went into the soft clay.

Later, Sabrina wasn't conscious of how much time had passed, her father knocked once on the door and opened it. She didn't have time to wipe the river of tears from her face, so she kept her back to the door.

'We're leaving now,' he told her. 'Don't forget your promise. Eat and straight to bed.'

'Yes, Dad,' she answered tightly. 'Have a good time.'

The interruption checked the onslaught of tears. She suddenly realized how drained she was, emotionally and physically. When the front door leading to the stairwell to the street closed, signaling the departure of her father and Deborah, Sabrina sank on to the work stool. She tiredly buried her face in her hands, not wanting to move or expend the energy to breathe.

A pounding began. For an instant she thought it was coming from inside her head. Then she realized it was coming from the stairwell door downstairs. She grimaced wryly as she rubbed her cheeks dry.

'Dad must have forgotten his key,' she muttered aloud, and slipped off the stool.

Her legs refused to be hurried as she made her way out of the studio and down the stairs to the second floor. The knocking continued, more demanding than before.

'I'm coming!' Irritation raised her voice and the sound stopped.

The muscles at the back of her neck had become knotted with tension and she rubbed them wearily as she turned the automatic lock and opened the door.

'What's the matter? Did you forget your key?' She tried to make her voice sound light and teasing, but it was a hollow attempt. Her greeting was met with silence. Sabrina tilted her head to the side in a listening attitude. 'Dad?'

'Did you know there's a smudge of clay on your cheek?'

Sabrina recoiled instinctively from the sound of Bay's voice. Her hand moved to shut the door, but he blocked it effectively and stepped into the room.

'How did you get up here? What do you want?' she demanded angrily.

'I met your father and Deborah on their way out. He let me in,' he explained calmly.

'Why?' She pivoted away, unable to face him, a hand nervously wiping the clay from her cheek.

'Why did he let me in?' Bay questioned. 'He said something about you working too hard.'

'Well, I'm not!' she said emphatically. 'And I meant why did you come?'

'To ask you to have dinner with me.'

'No.' Sabrina tipped her head back, her lashes fluttering down in a silent prayer to be left alone.

'I won't accept that,' he stated. 'You have to eat, and it might as well be with me as alone.'

'You'll have to accept it, because I'm busy. It doesn't bother me in the least to eat alone.' A solitary meal was something she had better get used to, she told herself.

'Sabrina, stop being stubborn,' Bay admonished calmly. 'There's no need to change clothes. Just take off your smock and go as you are. We'll eat and I'll bring you directly back here to finish your work, if it's essential it be done tonight.'

'I'm not going to be talked into going,' she warned.

With a fluid step, Bay reached out and untied the sash of her smock. Quickly she tried to tie the bow again, but his fingers closed over her wrist to prevent it.

'You are not going to bully me this time, Bay Cameron,' Sabrina muttered, straining to free her wrist from his grasp.

He held it easily. 'It's going to be a long night, because I'm not leaving here until you agree.'

It was not an idle threat. He was just arrogant enough to carry it out. The fire spreading through her arm was a second threat, a threat that she might not be able to hide her feelings or hold her tongue if she tried to outwait him.

Sabrina closed her mouth tightly for a moment. 'If I agree to this blackmail of yours, do I have your word that from now on you will accept my decisions about going with you as final?'

Her request was met by guarded silence for long seconds. 'You have my word, if,' there was an edge of fine steel in his voice, '*if you* will agree that we will discuss the reason for your sudden animosity.'

'I don't know what you're talking about,' she said coolly. Her heart started pounding frantically.

'Your word, Sabrina,' Bay ignored her denial.

The sigh she released was a well disguised checked sob. 'All right, you have it. Now let go of me.' Her wrist was freed. She rubbed the tender area unconsciously. 'But I still don't know what you're talking about,' she lied.

Her attitude toward him had changed, but not for anything did she want him to discover why. Pity because she was blind was one thing, but pity because she loved him was something she refused to tolerate.

'We'll see,' Bay murmured quietly.

How she hated his air of confidence! Sabrina flung her smock in the general direction of a chair and stalked to the umbrella stand to get her cane, the ivory cane that Bay had given her.

'Let's go, so we can get this over with,' she declared.

'Aren't you forgetting your bag?' he mocked. 'You might need your key to get back in unless — you plan to spend the night with me.'

'Perish the thought!' Sabrina spat.

But the thought was pure torture stabbing into her heart as she hurried up the stairs to her room. It hurt that Bay could joke about making love to her, especially when it was something that she wanted so very much.

Downstairs with her purse in hand, she brushed past him through the door, ignoring his mocking, 'Are you ready now?'

Her continued silence in the car was for her own protection, not a desire to be rude. She couldn't begin to guess Bay's reasons for not speaking. He was an enigma. She didn't understand why he did anything he did. For instance, why did he want her company when she had made it obvious that she didn't want his?

Poignantly Sabrina realized that this was probably the last time she would be with Bay, if he kept his word. It was really impossible and impractical to keep going out with him when she knew the truth of her feelings. It would only bring more pain.

She knew he hoped to change her mind and persuade her to continue their relationship. He had succeeded the last time when she hadn't been aware of her love. Naturally he was sure that he could do it again — why, she didn't know. She had to guard against his charm. She mustn't prolong the time when they separated.

Her thoughts were centered on the man behind the wheel. Nothing else around her penetrated her consciousness. She couldn't hear the traffic. Up or down a San Francisco street, it didn't matter. She could not care less where he was taking her, although at some future time she would probably think of the restaurant with pain.

'Sabrina.'

The faint command for her attention drew her out of the sheltering cocoon of her misery. She sat up straighter, realizing with a start that they had stopped. The engine had been turned off. Pink heightened her cheekbones, but she knew the dimness of the car concealed it.

'Are we here?' She tipped her head to a haughty angle.

'Yes,' Bay answered.

Her fingers closed tightly around her cane while she waited for Bay to walk around the car to open her door. The serpent heads carved into the ivory handle left an imprint in her fingers. Since she didn't know where she was going, she had to accept the guidance of his hand at her elbow. Several paces farther, he opened a door and ushered her into a building.

Footsteps immediately approached them and a woman's voice greeted them in pleasant surprise. 'You're here already, sir. Let me take your coat.'

Bay shrugged out of a light topcoat. 'Yes, it didn't take me as long as I thought, Mrs. Gibbs. Mrs. Gibbs, I'd like you to meet Sabrina Lane. Sabrina, this is Mrs. Gibbs.'

'How do you do, Mrs. Gibbs,' Sabrina greeted the woman warily, her ears straining to hear the sounds familiar to a restaurant.

'I'm pleased to meet you, Miss Lane.' Then the footsteps retreated.

'What kind of a restaurant is this?' Sabrina whispered, not certain if anyone could overhear.

'It's not a restaurant.' His hand was at her elbow again, leading her forward.

'But —' Sabrina frowned.

'This is my home, Sabrina,' Bay stated calmly.

She stopped abruptly. 'You said you were taking me out to eat,' she accused.

'But I never said to a restaurant.' He released her elbow and curved his arm around the back of her waist, propelling her forward. 'And you never asked.'

Sabrina twisted away from his arm. 'You've tricked me for the last time, Bay Cameron.' Her voice trembled with emotion. 'You can just turn around and take me home right now.'

'I gave Mrs. Gibbs a list of your favorite things. She's gone to a great deal of trouble to cook a meal you'll like. She'll be very disappointed if you don't stay.'

'You were never concerned about my feelings,' she reminded him sharply. 'Why should I worry about hurting hers?'

'Because essentially you're a gentle and sensitive woman and because,' his low voice became ominously soft, 'you gave me your word.'

'And I'm supposed to honor it even when you don't keep yours.' Sabrina swallowed back a helpless sob of frustration.'

'I've never lied to you.'

'No, you've only tricked, maneuvered and bullied me into doing what you want, but after all, you are Bay Cameron. You can make up your own code of ethics, can't you?' she snapped sarcastically.

'Shall we go into the living room?' A fine thread of cold steel ran through his voice and Sabrina knew her barbs had pricked.

Paradoxically she felt remorse and satisfaction at hurting him. She loved him desperately, but she hated him, too, for seeing her only as an unfortunate blind girl and not as a woman with physical and emotional needs. She didn't oppose the arm that firmly guided her forward. They turned at right angles and his steps slowed.

'Why did you bring me here, Bay?' Sabrina challenged coldly.

'We couldn't spend the evening in the hallway,' he answered, deliberately misunderstanding her question.

'You know very well I was referring to your home,' she accused.

'It offered privacy for the talk we're going to have.'

'Privacy could be obtained in your car, or for that matter at my house,' Sabrina reminded him.

'They wouldn't do. In a car, you could lose your temper and possibly jump out the door before I could stop you and be run down by some passing motorist,' Bay explained logically. 'Your home wouldn't work either. You know it better than the back of your hand. As stubborn as you can be sometimes, I would probably have found myself talking to the door of some room you'd locked yourself into. Here, in my home, you don't know which way to move without running the risk of falling over furniture or banging into a wall.'

'And you wonder why I've suddenly begun to dislike you!' Sabrina protested, spinning away, but unable to move with any swiftness.

He had laid the trap too cleverly. The end of her cane raced out to search for any obstacles in front of her and banged against a solid object.

'The sofa is directly in front of you. There's a chair to your right,' he said. 'Take one step backward and turn to your right and you'll avoid the chair.'

'What's in the way after that?' she asked caustically.

'Why don't you see for yourself?'

Slowly Sabrina followed his instructions, putting distance between them as she crossed an empty space with the aid of her cane. Finally the ivory white tip touched what appeared to be a table leg. She carefully sidestepped around it only to find the table had been sitting against a wall. Or at least, it was something solid, maybe a door. Sabrina reached out with her hand to investigate, and sheer filmy curtains met her fingers.

'The window overlooks San Francisco Bay.' His voice came from the center of the room. 'There's an unobstructed view of the Golden Gate and the Harbor.'

Sabrina didn't know what she had hoped to discover, a way out, possibly. Frustrated, she turned away from the window and partially retraced her steps, stopping before she came too near the area where she guessed that he would be.

'Bay, take me home, please,' she asked softly.

'Not yet.'

The carpet was soft and thick beneath her feet. She wondered at its color, the type of furnishing that surrounded her. There was a desire to explore this place where he lived and slept. She shook her head firmly. She mustn't think about that.

'If you don't take me home, I'll just call a cab.' She raised her chin defiantly.

'Where's the telephone, Sabrina? Do you know?' mocked Bay. Averting her face from the watchfulness of his eyes, she released a frantic, sobbing sigh. 'What's troubling you, Sabrina?'

'You're virtually holding me prisoner in this house and you have the nerve to ask why I'm upset!' she cried angrily.

'There's more to it than that and I mean to find out what it is.'

His voice was moving closer, the plushness of the carpet muffling his steps. Sabrina turned to face him, trying to use her sensitive radar to pinpoint his location.

'Maybe I'm tired of being treated like a child,' she suggested icily.

'Then stop acting like one!' Bay snapped.

With a start, she discovered he was closer than she had realized. His hands touched her shoulders, but before his fingers could dig into her flesh, she shied quickly away.

'For God's sake, Sabrina, why are you afraid of me?' he demanded. 'Every time I come near you now you tremble like a frightened rabbit. You've been like this ever since Pamela's party. Is that what upset you? Why you're afraid to let me near you?'

Her breathing was shallow and uneven. 'It didn't inspire me to trust you.' Sabrina lashed back, unable to explain that it had precipitated the discovery that she was in love with him.

'I was angry. I never meant to frighten you,' Bay said forcefully. This time his hands closed over her shoulders before she could elude them. His touch was firm but not bruising.

'Isn't it a little late to be regretting it now?' She lowered her chin so he couldn't see into her face as she made the sarcastic retort. 'We can't be friends, Bay, not any more.'

'Then I'll undo the damage,' came his low, clipped response.

He pulled her toward him. Her hands automatically pushed against the solidness of his chest. It was the last resistance Sabrina offered as his mouth closed over hers. It took all of her strength and will to keep from responding to the persuasive mastery of his kiss. At all costs she had to prevent him from discovering the effect he had on her. He mustn't know the fiery leap of desire in her loins that nearly made her limp in his arms.

The kiss seemed to go on for ever. Sabrina didn't know how much longer she could hold back the raging fire Bay had started. Before the shuddering sigh of surrender escaped, he dragged his mouth from her throbbing lips.

'Sabrina.' The husky, whispering tautness of his caressing voice was very nearly the final blow.

Her heart had a stranglehold on her throat, but she forced the words of rejection through. 'Now, will you let me go?' she demanded in a strained voice.

'What is it, Sabrina?' he asked guardedly. 'My kiss doesn't frighten you, nor my touch. I don't think you're frightened of anything, but there's something wrong, some explanation why you don't want to continue to see me.'

She stood silently for a minute, realizing he was not going to free her immediately. Sabrina took a deep breath and tossed back her head. She was about to make the biggest bluff in her life and the most important.

'Do you want the truth, Bay?' she challenged boldly. 'Well, the truth is that when you first met me I was lost and lonely. I was nothing and my destination was nowhere. You pushed me out of my shell and gave me companionship. More important, you gave me back a chance for a career in a field I love more than anything else in the world. I'll always be eternally grateful to you for that.'

She paused for an instant, feeling his stillness. 'I wish you hadn't forced me to say this, Bay. I don't mean to be unkind, but I'm not lost or lonely any more. I have my career and a goal, and that's all I ever wanted in life. I've enjoyed the times we spent together. But you tend to dominate and the only thing I want to dominate my life is my work. To sum it all up in one sentence, I simply don't need you any more.'

'I see.' His hands fell away from her shoulders as he stepped away. His voice was cuttingly grim. 'I don't think you could have put it more clearly.'

'It was never my intention, consciously or unconsciously, to use you, I hope you'll believe that,' Sabrina explained. 'About two weeks ago I realized that I wanted to devote all of my time to my work, but I didn't know how to tell you that without sounding ungrateful for all you'd done. All you were asking in return was a casual friendship, and I was too selfish to even want to give you that. So I tried to pick a fight with you, thinking that if you became angry, you might be the one to break it off. I'm sorry, Bay.'

A tear slipped from her lashes at the magnitude of her lie. Nothing was further from the truth, but his silence told her that he believed her.

'Would you mind taking me home, Bay?' she requested, her voice choked with pain.

'I don't think either one of us has much of an appetite,' he agreed bitterly. 'It really isn't very surprising.'

An impersonal hand took her elbow. Not another word was spoken. Bay made no comment on the tears that ran freely down her checks. He didn't even tell her goodbye when he saw her to the door, but his sardonic 'good luck' echoed in Sabrina's ears all the way to her room where she sprawled on to the bed and cried.

Ten

'Sabrina! Would you come downstairs a minute?' Grant Lane called from the base of the stairs.

She sighed heavily. 'Can't it wait?'

'No, it's important,' was the answer.

Reluctantly Sabrina covered the lump of clay just beginning to take shape. If she had persisted, she probably could have persuaded her father to postpone whatever it was that was so important, but she was simply too tired to argue. In the last two weeks, she had worked hard and slept little.

'I'll be right down,' she said as she forced her legs to carry out her statement. 'What did you want, Dad?' Halfway down the stairs, she felt a prickling along the back of her neck. For a few steps, she blamed the sensation on strain and tired nerves. She stopped abruptly on the last step, her head jerking towards the stairwell door.

'Hello, Sabrina. I apologize for interrupting your work.' The sardonic derision in Bay's tone cut her to the quick.

Blanching slightly, Sabrina dropped her chin, taking the last step and shoving her trembling hands in her pocket. 'What a surprise, Bay,' her own voice sounded anything but delighted. 'What brings you here?'

'Bay stopped to —' her father began to explain.

'You might call it my last good deed,' Bay interrupted blandly. 'I want you to meet Howell Fletcher, Sabrina.'

'This is the young lady you've been telling me about?' a cultured, masculine voice said, stepping forward to greet her. 'Miss Lane, I hope this is a pleasure, for both of us.'

Bewildered, Sabrina offered her hand. It was gripped lightly by smooth fingers and released. 'I'm sorry, I don't think I understand,' she apologized.

'Howell is here to see your work and give his considered opinion on your talent and potential,' Bay explained. The total lack of warmth in his voice almost made him seem like a stranger. There was none of the gentle mockery or friendliness she was accustomed to hearing.

'I don't think —' Sabrina started to protest stiffly that she didn't believe she was ready to have her work criticized by a professional.

'You might as well find out now whether or not you're wasting your time or building false hopes,' the man identified as Howell Fletcher stated.

'Good deed' — that was what Bay had said his motive was. Sabrina couldn't help wondering if he wasn't wishing she would fall flat on her face.

'I keep all my work in the studio upstairs.' Her chin lifted proudly. 'Are you coming, Bay?'

'No, I won't be staying.' The outcome apparently mattered little to him as he took his leave of her father and Howell Fletcher. Sabrina he ignored.

Robotlike, Sabrina led Howell Fletcher to the studio. The man spoke not one word while he slowly studied each piece, but she didn't mind. Strangely she didn't care what his opinion was. There was only one man who mattered, and Bay had walked in and out before her broken heart could start beating again.

Her work was a way of filling the empty, lonely hours, providing a challenge and a reason to get up each morning. Some day, she hoped her labors would allow her to be independent of her father. She wanted him to marry Deborah and be happy. It was only right that one of them should have the person they loved. She would never have Bay.

'How much of this work have you done since you became blind, Miss Lane?' the man asked thoughtfully.

'In clay? All of it,' she answered absently. 'The paintings were done before my accident.'

'I understood that you've only known Mr. Cameron for a few months,' he commented.

'Yes, that's right.' Sabrina wearily rubbed the back of her neck.

'How did you manage to do this bust?'

A wry smile curved her mouth. 'A blind person sees with their hands, Mr. Fletcher.'

'You haven't asked what I think yet. Aren't you curious, Miss Lane?'

'It's always been my experience that criticism comes without asking and compliments come without,' she shrugged dryly.

'You have a remarkable amount of wisdom,' he commented.

'Not in all things.' Not in loving wisely.

Then Howell Fletcher began to talk, more correctly to criticize. He didn't temper his words but sliced them into her, uncaring that it was her future he was cutting away. He dissected each piece. Every flaw, no matter how minute, was called to her attention. Each object was pushed into her hands so she could examine it for herself.

On and on the cultured voice droned until Sabrina wanted to cry out for him to stop. The weight of failure began to hunch her shoulders, trying to ward off the final, crushing blow. Her face, already haunted by the torture of unrequited love, became bleaker. Pride kept her chin up as the last piece was disposed of with the same analytical surgery as the others. A heavy silence followed his statement.

'Well,' Sabrina breathed in deeply, 'I never realized I was such an incompetent amateur.'

'My God, child,' the critic laughed, 'you're not incompetent nor an amateur. Some of the pieces are clumsy, the inanimate ones that need work on the flow of their line. But the others are stunning. The pride and power that you've stamped in Bay's face is unbelievable. The pathos of the madonna-like figure is touching in the extreme. Like your paintings, your talent lies in people. You bring them to life, heighten the qualities that attract people.'

'Then,' she couldn't believe she was hearing him correctly, 'you think I should keep working?'

'If you can keep up this pace and this standard, I can promise you a showing within six months,' Howell Fletcher declared.

'You must be joking,' Sabrina breathed.

'My dear, I never joke about money. And if you'll pardon me saying so, your blindness is going to attract a great deal of beautiful publicity. What we will do is combine a display of your very best paintings with the very best clay models and start out with an invitation-only showing for all the "right" people —' The plans continued to spew forth long after the shock of his announcement wore off.

'You aren't saying this because of Bay, are you?' Sabrina interrupted, suddenly afraid that Bay had exerted his influence to arrange this.

'Are you asking me if I was bribed to tell you this?' he demanded, sounding indignantly affronted. She nodded hesitantly. 'Bay Cameron did apply pressure to bring me here today, but I would never risk my reputation for anyone! If you had neither talent nor potential, I would have told you so in no uncertain terms.'

Sabrina believed him. The victory cup of success was within her grasp. She let the man issue forth his plans, knowing that the nectar from the cup did not taste sweet because she couldn't share it with the man she loved. The triumph was as hollow as she was.

A private show within six months, Howell Fletcher had declared. After careful consideration, he had pushed the date ahead to the first week of December, timing it for the holiday season and loosened purse strings. Sabrina had silently realized that his appreciation of art went hand in hand with his appreciation of money.

'I think you've done it, Sabrina,' her father murmured so he couldn't be overheard by the people milling about. 'All I've heard is one compliment after another.'

Sabrina smiled faintly, not at his words of success but at the deep pride in his voice. She could imagine the beaming smile on his face.

'Words of praise are cheap, Mr. Lane,' Howell Fletcher put in from the other side of Sabrina, but there was triumph in his tone. 'You're a success, my dear Sabrina, because our guests are putting their money where their mouth is, to put it crudely.'

'Thanks to you, Howell,' she said softly.

'Always the diplomat,' he chided. 'It took both of our talents, as you very well know. Now, I must circulate. You stay here and look beautiful.'

'Sabrina.' A warm, female voice called her name, followed by the floral scent of violets. 'It's me, Pamela Thyssen. You were at my home some months ago.'

'Of course, Mrs. Thyssen, I remember you very well.' Sabrina extended her hand and had it clasped by beringed fingers. 'How are you?'

'A little upset, if you must know,' the woman scolded mockingly. 'It was dreadful of you not to volunteer any information about your remarkable talent. And wait until I get my hands on Bay. I'll teach that godson of mine a lesson or two for keeping me in the dark.'

'At the time, there wasn't anything to tell.' She swallowed nervously. Every time his name was mentioned her heart started skipping beats and an icy cold hand would close around her throat.

'I should think Bay would be here tonight, helping you to celebrate your success. Surely he could have cut short his sailing trip to Baja for an occasion like this,' Pamela stated.

'Oh, is that where he is?' Sabrina tried to sound unconcerned. 'I haven't seen him lately. I've been so busy getting ready for this show and all.'

Pamela Thyssen obviously wasn't aware that she and Bay had parted company several months ago. Sabrina didn't intend to enlighten her either.

'The bust you did of him is positively stealing the show. Everyone is talking about how remarkable the likeness is,' the woman observed in a faintly curious tone. 'Howell must have realized how successful it would be, judging by the price he put on it.'

'I'm merely the artist.' Sabrina shrugged to indicate that she had nothing to do with the price of the items.

She had not wanted to exhibit the bust at all, but Howell had been adamant in his arguments, insisting that she could not allow sentiment to color her judgment. When she had finally given in, it was with the proviso that the bust would not be for sale.

That was when she learned that Howell Fletcher's shrewdness was not limited to money and art. He had asked if she wanted to raise speculation as to why it wasn't for sale. It would be better, he suggested, to put an exorbitant price tag on it, too high for anyone to purchase it. Sabrina had finally agreed.

'What was Bay's reaction when he saw the model you did of him?' Pamela inquired.

One of the other guests chose that moment to offer his congratulations and comments and Sabrina was able to ignore the question. A few others stopped after that. Eventually Pamela was sidetracked by someone she knew and Sabrina was able to escape the question completely.

'It's stunning, Miss Lane,' a woman gushed. 'Absolutely stunning. The paintings, the statues, they're all so breathtakingly real.'

'Thank you,' Sabrina nodded politely, not knowing how to counter the effusiveness of the woman's praise.

'Excuse me, Mrs. Hamilton, but I must steal Sabrina away from you for a moment,' Howell Fletcher broke in, a smooth hand tucking itself under Sabrina's elbow.

Sabrina offered her apologies to the woman and gratefully allowed Howell to guide her away. The ivory cane tapped its way in front of her. She had learned that Howell often forgot she was blind and let her run into things.

'Who are you spiriting me off to see this time?' she asked, wiping a damp palm on the skirt of her black dress.

'I don't know how to tell you this exactly, Sabrina.' Apprehension echoed in his cautious statement. 'We have a buyer for the bust, and he wants to see you.'

'A buyer?' She stiffened. 'You know it's not for sale.'

'I tried to explain that you were very reluctant to part with it, that its real worth was something less than the price. I couldn't very well tell him how much less for fear the information would get around and the other prices would be questioned,' he replied defensively.

'I shouldn't have been persuaded to display it in the first place. You guessed how I felt about it,' she accused.

'Yes, I did,' he agreed quietly. 'Perhaps you can appeal to his better nature and persuade him to choose something else. He's waiting in my office. It will afford some privacy for the discussion.'

'I'm not going to sell it,' Sabrina stated emphatically as they left behind most of the guests to enter a back hall. 'I don't care what the repercussions are.'

Howell didn't comment, slowing her down and turning her slightly as he reached around to open the door. She walked into the room with a determined lift of her chin. There was a quietly murmured 'good luck' from Howell and he closed the door. She turned back, startled, expecting to have his support.

Then she heard someone rise to his feet. She had been in the office many times and knew the potential buyer had been sitting on the Victorian sofa against the left wall. Fixing a bright smile on her face, she stepped toward the sound.

'How do you do,' Sabrina extended a hand in greeting. 'I'm Sabrina Lane. Howell told me you were interested in purchasing a particularly favorite piece of mine.'

'That's right, Sabrina.'

The voice went through her like a bolt of lightning. Her hand fell to her side as she fought to remain composed. The floor seemed to roll madly beneath her feet, but it was only her shaking knees.

'Bay — Bay Cameron,' she identified him with a breathless catch in the forced gaiety of her voice. 'What a coincidence! Pamela Thyssen was just telling me a few moments ago that you were on a sailing trip somewhere around Baja, California. It must be difficult to be in two places at once.'

Howell, that traitor, why hadn't he warned her that it was Bay who was waiting for her? No wonder he had sneaked away, leaving her alone!

'It was a natural mistake for Pamela to make. I hadn't planned to return for some time,' he replied in that impersonal tone that made her feel cold. 'Tonight you've achieved the success you wanted. How does it feel?'

Miserable, her heart answered. 'Splendid,' her voice lied.

'You're looking very chic and sophisticated in your dress of mourning black. The single strand of pearls around your long neck is a nice simple touch. The two make your complexion pale and hauntingly beautiful as if you've suffered great tragedy and risen above it. The press must be having a field day with your story,' Bay commented cynically.

She longed to tell him that her tragedy had been in losing him and not her sight, but she kept silent, trying not to hear the sarcasm underlining his voice.

'I would have thought by now you would have discarded the cane in favor of another.' The reference to the ivory carved handle in her hands made her grasp it more tightly as if afraid he would try to take it back.

'Why should I? It serves its purpose,' she shrugged nervously.

'I wasn't going to accuse you of attaching any sentimental importance to it,' Bay responded dryly. 'Although when I saw the bust you did of me, I was curious to find out if you look back on our association with fondness.'

'Naturally.' Her voice vibrated with the depth of her fondness. 'Besides, I told you once before that I liked your face. The features are strong and proud.'

'Howell did tell you that I'm going to buy it, didn't he?'

'Yes, but I never realized you were an egotist, Bay.' Her laughter was brittle. 'Imagine buying an image of yourself!'

'It will be an excellent reminder for the future.'

'Bay, I —' Sabrina pivoted slightly to the side, feeling the play of his eyes over her profile, cold and chilling. 'Th-there's been a mistake. Howell came to get me because . . . well, because it isn't for sale.'

'Why not?' He didn't sound upset by her stammering announcement. 'I thought the purpose of this show was to sell what was on display.'

'It is, but not this piece,' she protested. 'That's why we put the price so high, so no one would buy it.'

'I'm buying it,' Bay answered evenly.

'No! I'm not letting you have it!' She lashed out sharply in desperation. 'You've taken everything else from me. Please let me keep this!'

'Taken from you!' he laughed harshly. His hand snaked out to wrap his fingers around her wrist. 'What have I ever taken from you? Aren't you forgetting that I'm the one who was used? Why not take my money? You've taken everything else of value I had to give!'

'Pity? Sympathy? Charity?' The end of her cane tapped the floor sharply in punctuation to her angry words. 'When were those humiliating things ever of value? And to whom? Certainly not to me! You never cared about me! Not really! I was only a charity case to you!'

'You don't still believe I felt sorry for you?' A weary sigh came from deep within.

'You certainly don't love me,' Sabrina sniffed.

'And if I had,' his hand closed firmly on the back of her neck, turning her stiffly composed face toward him, 'would it have made any difference?'

If only he hadn't touched her, Sabrina thought, a fiery trail racing down her spine, maybe she could have withstood the agony tearing at her heart. Now she felt herself go limp inside, pride unable to support her, and she swayed against his chest.

'If you'd loved me just a little, Bay,' she sighed wistfully, inhaling the spicy fragrance clinging to his jacket, 'I might not have minded loving you so desperately. But what girl wants to be with a man who only pities her because she can't see?'

'You are blind, Sabrina,' he said. A great weight seemed to leave his voice. The hand slipped from her neck to the back of her waist while the other hand gently stroked her cheek. 'I never pitied you. I was too busy falling in love with you to waste time with that emotion.'

'Oh, Bay, don't tease me,' she cried in anguish, twisting free from his tender embrace. 'Haven't I shamed myself enough without having you make fun of me?'

'I'm not teasing. Believe me, the hell I've been going through these last months hasn't been funny at all,' Bay stated.

'I'm blind, Bay. How could you possibly love me?' she pleaded with him to stop tormenting her.

'My brave and beautiful blind queen, how could I possibly not love you?' His tone was incredibly warm and caressing. The sincerity of it almost frightened Sabrina.

'You aren't trying to trick me again, are you, Bay? Don't do this to me if all you want is the bust I did of you. I'll give it to you gladly if it will make you stop lying.'

A pair of hands closed over her shoulders and she was drawn against his chest. He placed her hands on his heart, rapidly thudding against her palm. Her own heart had to race wildly to keep in tempo. Cupping her face in his hands, Bay bestowed soft kisses on her closed eyes.

'Being blind doesn't make you feel less of a woman when I hold you in my arms, darling,' he whispered tightly.

'You never let me guess, not once,' Sabrina murmured, leaning her head weakly against his heart.

'I wanted to a hundred times in a hundred ways.' Strong arms held her close as if afraid she would try to escape again. 'I loved you almost from the beginning. Maybe it started that night we took refuge from the rain in my boat. I don't know. But I told myself I had to take it slow. You were proud, stubborn, defensive and very insecure. I didn't try to convince you in the beginning that I was in love with you, because you wouldn't have believed me. That's why I set about trying to help you build confidence in yourself. I wanted you to learn that there was nothing you couldn't do if you set your mind to it. Arrogantly I thought after that was accomplished I would make you fall in love with me. You can imagine what a blow it was to my self-esteem when you informed me that you didn't need me any more.'

He smiled against her temple and Sabrina snuggled closer. 'I needed you. I wanted you desperately,' she murmured fervently. 'I was terrified you would guess and feel even sorrier for me.'

'I never felt pity. Pride, but never pity.'

'Pride?' She turned her face toward him, questioning and bewildered.

'I was always proud of you. No matter what challenge I made, you always accepted it.' Lightly he kissed her lips.

'Accepted with protest,' she reminded him with an impish smile.

'No one could ever accuse you of being tractable. Stubborn and independent, yes, but never tractable. You made that plain the first time we met and you slapped my face,' Bay laughed softly.

'And you slapped me back.' Sabrina let her fingertips caress his cheek. 'It made me angry. Eventually it made me love you.'

His fingers quickly gripped her hand and stopped the caressing movement, pressing a hard kiss in her palm. 'Will you tell me now why you ran away from me at Pamela's?' he demanded huskily. 'The truth this time.'

Her heart skipped a beat. At the moment she didn't want to talk, not after the sensually arousing kiss in her sensitive palm.

'I heard you talking to a girl named Roni. She said you'd brought me with you because you felt sorry for me and because you hoped to make her jealous. You didn't deny it, Bay. I kept hoping you would at least say I was your friend, but you just let her keep rattling on about me being a charity case and a poor unfortunate. I thought she was telling the truth. That's why I ran away,' she admitted.

She heard and felt the rolling chuckle that vibrated from deep within. It was throaty and warm and strangely reassuring.

'One of the first things I'm going to have to remember when we're married is how acute your hearing is,' Bay declared with a wide smile of satisfaction against her hair. 'If you'd eavesdropped a little longer, you would have heard me tell Roni to take a flying leap at the moon and that I didn't appreciate her comments about the woman I was going to marry.'

'Bay!' Her voice caught for a moment on the tide of love that welled in her throat. 'Are you going to marry me?'

'If that's a proposal, I accept.'

'D-don't tease,' she whispered with a painful gasp.

His mouth closed over hers in a tender promise. Instantly Sabrina responded, molding herself tightly against every hard male curve. Hungry desire blazed in his deepening kiss as he parted her lips to savor every inch of her mouth. His love lit a glowing lamp that chased away all the shadows of her dark world.

Long heady moments later Bay pushed her unsteadily out of his arms. She swayed toward his chest rising and falling so unevenly beneath her fingers. His hands rigidly held her at a distance.

'Darling, I love you so,' Sabrina whispered achingly. 'Please hold me a little while longer.'

'I'm not made of iron, my love.' The sternness of his voice only indicated the deepness of his love. 'A little while longer would be too long.'

The corners of her wide mouth were tugged upward in a tiny smile of immense pleasure. 'The door has a lock, Bay.'

'And there's a horde of people who must be wondering what's happened to the star of the show,' he reminded her tersely.

'I don't want to be a star,' she answered.

'Your work —' Bay began.

'— will fill the moments you are away from me. That's all it will ever do for me,' Sabrina declared in a husky murmur.

'You're not making it easy to be sensible,' he growled, letting her come back into his arms.

'I know,' she whispered in the second before his mouth closed passionately over hers.

Biography

Janet Dailey

Janet Dailey was born Janet Haradon in 1944 in Storm Lake, Iowa. She attended secretarial school in Omaha, Nebraska before meeting her husband, Bill. Bill and Janet worked together in construction and land development until they "retired" to travel throughout the United States, inspiring Janet to write the Americana series of romances, where she set a novel in every state of the Union. In 1974, Janet Dailey was the first American author to write for Harlequin. Her first novel was NO QUARTER ASKED. She has since gone on to write approximately 90 novels, 21 of which have appeared on the New York Times Bestseller List. She has won many awards and accolades for her work, appearing widely on Radio and Television. Today, there are over three hundred million Janet Dailey books in print in 19 different languages, making her one of the most popular novelists in the world.

CPSIA information can be obtained at www.ICGtesting.com
Printed in the USA
LVOW060337151111

255029LV00001B/148/P